BACK HOME

W. L. Harvey

Publisher's note: This is a work of fiction. Names, characters, places, and incidents either are the product of the author's imagination or are used fictitiously. Any resemblance to actual events, locales, or persons, living or dead, is entirely coincidental.

Edited, formatted, and book design by Kristen Corrects, Inc.
Cover art design by XXXX

First edition published 2017

ISBN: 0692917861
ISBN 13: 9780692917862
Library of Congress Control Number: 2017911054
W. L. Harvey, Fayetteville, NC

CHAPTER ONE

*T*oday is a blessing. Today is a curse.
I don't know why this keeps coming to mind. Is it possible for a day to be both? Can I honestly look at myself and think that I am both blessed as well as cursed to be alive another day?

Too much deep thinking before I hit the road, Ben Martin thought.

His truck sat in the driveway. There were only a few more boxes to go before the house was empty of his belongings. *Funny thing*, he thought—*twenty years ago, all I had to my name could fit in a duffle bag, and in fact did fit in a duffle.* After two decades of military service and one failed marriage, his total belongings still didn't add up to much. It helped that after the divorce a lot of it had gone straight to Goodwill or in the trash. He had come to realize that there wasn't a lot of stuff in his life he really wanted to hang on to, mostly books and his camera. Clothes? He had some, basic man clothes: jeans, T-shirts, a couple of button-up shirts, nothing significant.

Kind of how he felt about his life. Nothing significant. Not a lot to point at and say, "There—there's my mark. There's proof that I existed and made a difference in this world." A folded flag (not made in China, thank God), a lapel pin, and a rubber-stamped certificate that reads *Your Nation Thanks You for Your Service.* Hell, now that he thought about it, it probably wasn't even rubber stamped—did people even use those anymore?

Ben carried the final box out to his truck. As he loaded it into the back, he thought about the last few days, his last in the Army.

Ben leaned against the bar, sipping occasionally from his beer. His eyes wandered the room, taking in the number of fellow soldiers who came to see him off. He had been the center of attention for the last couple of hours due to the ceremony inherent in a senior person's retirement, but now different groups had formed as the festivities wound down.

He watched as his former commanding officer, Jim Davies, approached with a beer in hand. He smiled as he neared Ben, and Ben smiled back.

"Nice party, Ben," Jim said. "And it's nice to be able to call you Ben outside of my office."

Ben had served his last year as Jim's first sergeant, and the two got along well. Ben liked Jim—he was one of the rare officers these days, the ones who realized that the non-commissioned officers actually run the Army. Jim stayed out of Ben's way, allowing Ben to conduct the unit's daily business while Jim handled the officer duties.

"Thanks for coming, sir," Ben said.

"So what's next?" Jim asked.

Ben laughed as he pondered this question. "Honestly? I'm a little unsure about that. I have a general idea but nothing specific, if that's what you're asking."

Jim frowned. "You've never struck me as a man without a plan, First Sergeant."

Ben turned to look at Jim. "Sir, you'll pardon me if I speak frankly, as I'll be a civilian soon." He took another sip. "After the last few years, my main goal is a little peace and quiet for a while. It's time for us old guys to take a step back, let these young'uns handle the war."

"Fair enough, Ben. I just figured you were going to stick around the area, get one of those high paying civilian jobs with the Army, get paid a lot of money telling the young soldiers how it was back in your day."

Ben laughed again. "I've had some offers…"

"So why not take one of them? You've been one of the best NCOs I've ever worked with. Why quit now?"

Ben looked at the young captain. "Oh, there's plenty more like me, sir."

Jim nodded. "So, if I may pry a little more, are you looking for that peace and quiet here in Fayetteville, or somewhere else?"

"Not here. My mother left me a place down in Mississippi, where I'm from. I'm going down there. I don't know if I'll stay, but right now I just need to get away from the Army."

As he spoke, Ben put his hand in his pocket, looking for the hard piece of plastic he had kept there for close to ten years now. Every day, he made sure he had it. It had become his talisman, a good luck piece. It was there, and it gave him comfort.

"Well, there isn't a soul alive who wouldn't say you haven't earned that right. Good on you, Ben. I just don't want you to take off without a plan. I've known you for a while now. You're not going down to Mississippi and turning into Thoreau, are you? Shunning the public, extolling the virtues of self-reliance, and turning into a hermit?"

Ben grinned. "You may not believe this, but I've read Thoreau. For all his talk of getting away from it all and back to nature, he was a mama's boy who ate supper at her house while she did his laundry."

3

They shared another laugh. "I wish you all the luck in the world, and you know where you can find me if you need anything." Jim offered his hand. "And give me a shout if you win the lottery or something; I could use the money."

Ben took it, gave it a firm shake. "Sir, I appreciate it, I do. I'm looking forward to some relaxing times. I don't play the lottery anymore," he added. "What would I do with a lot of money? Buy a lot of crap I really don't need."

⚜

Ben stood in the driveway and waited on someone to tell him what to do. When no one presented themselves to offer any advice or direction, he got in his truck and left. He didn't look back.

⚜

As Ben pulled away, Jamie thought to himself, *Oh good, the dude is finally leaving. Maybe he'll do something that's worth reporting.*

The inside of his car smelled terrible—why did they always leave that part out in the movies? A pungent mixture of farts, corn chips, and coffee permeated the interior, plus a healthy dose of body odor to top it off.

Jamie had been observing Ben for two weeks now. He rented a hotel room outside of Fayetteville that rented by the week, but he was rarely there. Classy place, too—the three times he had returned to bathe he had been propositioned for sex twice and what he was told was high quality weed, get you good with the *Lord,* brother. Each time he politely declined.

He watched Ben turn off the street and drive toward the interstate. He fumbled for his phone, sent a text, and waited. A message immediately came back telling him what to do. He slowly eased onto the road behind Ben and followed.

CHAPTER TWO

Stephen sat at one of the café tables on the sidewalk watching people walk by. One of his favorite things to do, actually—he always felt you could learn so much just by observing how people conduct themselves in public. That, and he also felt he was in one of the greatest places on earth to people watch if you were a healthy male.

The women. Dark, light, inviting, exotic, alluring, divine. He fell in love every five seconds just watching them. Not in a perverted or lustful manner—just from a simple appreciation of beauty. These women, he thought, knew how to present themselves in public. It was rare in this city to see a woman *not* made up, properly dressed to go out among the population. Not the way American women dressed, in his opinion—he thought the ladies in the United States were, for the most part, *trying* not to be presentable—wearing pajamas and sweats everywhere. Not *ladies*, in other words. Slobs. The men too. No one dressed...*nice*. When did going out unpresentable become socially acceptable?

No problem with that here. Not here, in the greatest city in the western hemisphere, according to him: Bogota, Colombia.

Of course, there are problems in a city with the history Bogota has, hence the heavily armed *policia* on every corner. He recalled that a few years back just down the street from his table, a couple of FARC nutcases had thrown a grenade into a restaurant that the gringos liked to frequent. No one had been seriously hurt—the restaurant had been mostly unoccupied during a slow part of the day—but it served to remind everyone that the Fuerzas Armadas Revolucionarias de Colombia was still around. The FARC didn't operate as much as they had in the past, though—what started out as a Communist movement to wrest power away from the government had devolved into a significant international drug cartel. Kidnapping also helped pay the bills, although the word had gone out a few years back: stop kidnapping gringos. Too much hassle and no one will pay.

Stephen sipped his coffee. He preferred to stay right here in the city—it was so much more civilized than the towns in the country. Cartagena wasn't too bad, or maybe Cali. Still, Bogota was where he felt the most comfortable. He also felt safer here, although that wasn't normally an issue—over the years he learned to blend in, to be a social chameleon, regardless of location. He was deeply tanned, trim, with graying dark brown hair and an unremarkable face that simply said "businessman" when he dressed in his normal suits. He easily passed as either European or a descendant of the Spaniards who had populated this country after mixing with the locals.

His phone beeped, indicating a text. Picking it up, he read the simple message: *He is leaving, do I follow?*

He typed, *Yes. Follow and advise of suspected destination if possible.*

He had a good idea of where the target was headed, but wanted to make sure. There was a lot riding on not necessarily the target's destination but also what the target intended to do once there. He sighed, thinking for a moment. *Do I let him go? Do I wait? If I move too soon, will everything fall apart?*

He drained his cup and tapped the phone number for the airline. "Hello? *Ingles, por favor.* Yes, I need to make a reservation for Atlanta."

CHAPTER THREE

The stretch of I-95 going south out of North Carolina is not that interesting to look at while driving. Without GPS, the best way to keep yourself oriented is to look at the South of the Border signs every mile or so telling you how far it is to discount fireworks and hats from around the world. As he rolled into South Carolina Ben thought, *Why have I never stopped here?*

Oh yes, I remember. Whenever I was going anywhere outside of North Carolina, the attraction was less than an hour into the journey, and upon returning I was less than an hour from the house, so why stop there?

Crossing the South Carolina state line (South of the Border right there on the left, in all its neon glory), Ben thought he was making good time. Leaving North Carolina felt…good? Sad? He had spent the better part of his twenty years in the Army there. In fairness, a lot of that time wasn't physically in the state—especially since Lauren had left, it was more of a place that he just kept his belongings rather than *home*.

When was the last time he had felt at home? He was told when he joined that the Army was now his home, no need to worry about that. Growing up, he was told that home was where he hung his hat. So…what was home, really? A house? Some land? A place where everyone knows you and accepts you? Where your family is? Is home a physical spot on a map, or simply a location where one felt safe?

He had transferred to Fort Bragg in 1995, and he and Lauren had first had an apartment after they married. Not good enough for her—eventually she wanted children, and an apartment just wouldn't do. A house outside of Fayetteville was their next place, and he liked it—there was a backyard, a garage in which to keep the rapidly accumulating military issue, and the neighbors were friendly. What else could a man want?

To Ben, it had been a good life. He was gone for training occasionally, but not for very long at a time. Things seemed to be going very well for them: Lauren got a job at an insurance firm in Fayetteville while going to medical school, and Ben gained a promotion to staff sergeant. He had just about reached the halfway point in his Army career when he needed to make the decision to stay or get out. There didn't appear to be a lot going on in the world, so he was looking at jobs outside the military.

On Tuesday, September 11, all of it changed. Ben was in the team room at his unit recovering after a ruck march the team had completed that morning. There was a hush over the unit as everyone watched the second plane fly into the World Trade Center in New York. Immediately after, the entire post was put on lockdown. Weapons with live ammunition were issued and everyone was assigned an area to guard. Ben sat with a loaded rifle and full kit near the Yadkin Road gate to Fort Bragg, wondering if anything was going to happen. Nothing did in the following days—seemed to him like they were slamming the barn door after the horses were already gone. He remembered all of it—the anger, the desire to *do something*. Lord knows that the years after that day in 2001 he would do plenty.

One more thing he did know that was going to happen: He was going to confront the asshole that had been following him for the better part of two weeks.

—═┼ ┼═—

Jamie had chosen the car he used carefully. After observing what people drove in Cumberland County, he picked a beat-up Chevrolet from the mid-nineties. No one would give it a second look, but it ran well. He hoped the car would blend in—most of the training he had received in surveillance had been conducted in gigantic black SUVs that screamed "WE ARE WATCHING YOU." This car didn't appear to be out of place anywhere.

He stayed about a mile behind Ben as they traveled on the interstate. Ben turned his blinker on once he reached I-20 to head west, and Jamie did the same.

—═┼ ┼═—

Ben glanced at his rear view mirror. *Yep, asshole is still there. Nice touch, staying that far back.* Of course, it wasn't hard to follow a blue 1985 Chevrolet Blazer. This kind of truck doesn't lend itself to low visibility travel. The truck was rare enough that he had received a few approving nods from male drivers on the interstate, plus a couple of female ones. The claymore mine trailer hitch also drew a few looks as well.

You know what? Let's see how far knucklehead wants to take this, he thought. *I've got nothing but time and miles to go.*

I-20 travels through South Carolina for almost 200 miles. South Carolina is quite pretty, but unfortunately the route the interstate takes doesn't give that impression too often—mostly fields and the usual interstate rest stop businesses, with the occasional promise of entertainment or historical significance announced via brown signs with white lettering. Ben thought that one day, when he had completely run out of things to do, he would drive from one end of the country to another just to visit all the places of historical value. There were plenty of them for a man with time on his hands.

Ben drove through Columbia, keeping his eye on the mirror to ensure the asshole following him was still there. The guy closed the distance somewhat once in Columbia proper, as traffic increased and it was more difficult to keep pace. Once on the west side of the city, the highway narrowed again to two lanes, and Ben spotted his tail dropping back a little.

Ben made his decision. The next exit he saw signs for had several gas stations, and more importantly, what looked like a state highway running perpendicular to the interstate. Without signaling, Ben jerked the steering wheel to the right just as the off ramp was passing his side. Ben continued down the ramp and turned right at the stop sign at the bottom.

Damn it. Jamie saw the Blazer lurch off the highway and onto the off ramp in a cloud of dust and gravel. Maybe Ben was daydreaming, realized he had to take a leak or something. As he approached the exit, he spotted the Blazer heading north, passing all the gas stations and fast food restaurants without stopping. *Maybe he knows he's being followed…?* No way, he had been too careful. *Let's see how this plays out.*

Jamie signaled to turn off the interstate and drove in the direction he saw the Blazer go.

As Ben drove, he opened his center console to retrieve his pistol. Keeping his eyes on the road, he manipulated the slide and glanced down quickly to ensure there was a round in the chamber. He had hoped that he would never need to use it again, but had to admit to himself that there was a slight feeling in the back of his mind that was getting happy about the prospect of action. Much of Ben's mind, though, was satisfied with the thought, *Better to have it and not need it than need it and not have it.* He had it.

⊱✦⊰

Where did that son of a bitch go? Jamie followed the state road past the gas stations and continued north, sweeping his gaze back and forth in search of the Blazer. He felt a sudden coldness in his stomach; he hoped he had not lost this guy.

There. Just off the highway, on a farm road leading off into the distance. The hood was up, and the driver's side door was open.

Don't want to make it too obvious, he thought. He drove past the road, braked, then reversed to the point where he could pull in behind the Blazer, about 100 feet off the highway. He put the car in park...and hesitated. He had a gun in the glove compartment. Should he take it? No. His job was to follow. This guy Ben had shown no indications that he had any idea he was being followed. Well, until he got off the interstate—but that could mean anything, right?

Jamie left the gun in the car and got out.

⊱✦⊰

Ben watched him approach through the crack between the hood and the cab of the truck. *Here we go,* he thought, pulling his pistol out of the waistband of his jeans and holding it behind his back.

"Having trouble?" he heard the man say as he walked up.

Ben smiled as he shut the hood. "No trouble at all, friend. Just heard a funny noise as I got away from the interstate. Wouldn't you know, I drove past all the gas stations first and *then* had trouble. Ain't that something?"

12

The man started to reply when Ben brought the pistol around. His eyes grew wide and he started to turn back to his car.

"Wouldn't do that if I were you," Ben said in a friendly tone. "Been a while since I shot anyone, but I'm pretty sure I could hit you from here."

The younger man stopped, then turned back toward Ben. His hands came up, and a resigned look came across his face. "What now?" he asked.

"Well, let's talk about that. First thing, who the hell are you and why are you following me?"

"Name's Jamie. Actually, James but everyone calls me Jamie."

"Okay, Jamie, now we got a name. That doesn't really tell me anything. Who are you?"

"Look, can we get this over with? You gonna shoot me or what?"

Ben looked down at the pistol in his hand, still pointed at Jamie's chest. He looked back up at Jamie.

"Hmm. That kind of depends. Are you intending to do me any harm?"

"No. I was hired to follow you and report, that's it. Nothing in my agreement about hurtin' you."

Ben made his decision. Safety on, pistol in small of back, tucked into his jeans. He spread his hands in a goodwill gesture. "There. Now no one is aimin' to hurt anyone. Just so you know, though, I can get at it pretty quick if I need to."

Jamie visibly relaxed.

"All right, what do you want to know?" Jamie asked.

"Let's start with who hired you to watch me."

"Any reason why I should?"

"I'm just asking, friend. Tell me or not, up to you."

Jamie leaned against the side of the Blazer. "You mind if I smoke?"

"Free country and all that."

Jamie pulled a cigarette from his pack and lit it with a butane lighter. After exhaling a plume of gray smoke, he looked at Ben.

"Honestly, I have no idea who wants you followed. I mean, I think I might have heard his name once, but all my instructions come through a burner phone. We never actually talk. I'm doing this because I needed money and the opportunity presented itself."

Ben said, "Okay, let's see the phone."

Jamie turned and walked back to the car, Ben right beside him. Ben still didn't fully trust this guy. Jamie sensed this and looked at Ben.

"I do have a gun in the glove compartment, but I wasn't going to use it unless there was trouble. Honest."

Ben thought for a second, then shrugged. "Good enough. You know my position on this."

Jamie opened the car door, slowly leaned in so Ben could see he wasn't trying to trick him, and picked up a small object lying on the passenger seat. He turned and handed it to Ben.

"There you go."

An older flip phone. Ben opened it and pushed the buttons to select the text message log. He read the messages, then flipped it shut and handed it back.

"See? That's it. I get a message, I do what it says."

Ben asked, "And you have no idea who this is on the other side?"

"Nope," Jamie replied. "I get a text, and like I said, I do what it tells me to do."

"Fine. Let's go back to how you started doing this then."

Jamie finished his cigarette and flicked it away. "I got out of the Army up at Bragg about four months ago. I did six years in the infantry, did one tour in Iraq and one in Afghanistan. I got shot in Afghanistan in 2012 and it fucked up my leg. Docs had to take it off at the knee. They said I could stay in and go to another job, but I really liked what I was doing—I had moved from a line company up to the reconnaissance platoon and enjoyed it a lot. That's where I got some surveillance training, some civilian guys who came and trained us for a week on urban stuff, counter-surveillance, driving, stuff like that."

Ben nodded, motioning him to continue.

"Well, the Army offered to medically discharge me and I took it. Man, I'm only twenty-five years old and all of a sudden I have no job. They do a decent job with prosthetics these days, you can see I hardly limp, took about a year and a half of physical therapy"—he walked a short distance to demonstrate—"but the powers that be decided that they didn't need me no more. So, I had two choices: I could go back home to Texas, or stay there in Fayetteville and find a job. I'm from one of those little towns in Texas where there ain't shit to do—hell, that's the reason I joined the Army in the first place—so I didn't want to go back home. Thing is, now that the wars are winding down there ain't hardly any jobs to be had as a government contractor, so I just crashed with a buddy of mine until I could find something."

Jamie paused to light another cigarette.

"About two months ago, after I had been to several job interviews and was seriously considering a career in fast food, another buddy of mine called me and said he might have something right up my alley. Just observation and reporting, nothing serious. Or so he said, anyway."

Jamie paused, his eyes far away as he remembered.

"I needed something. All I was doing was lying around, drinking too much, waiting on the next disability check to deposit so I could buy more beer and cigarettes. I helped the guy I was crashing with on his rent, but his wife was getting tired of me by this time, making a point of banging pots and pans around when I was asleep on the couch. Didn't really matter too much, to be honest; I wasn't sleeping too good anyway. Every time I closed my eyes all I could see was a muzzle flash, a lot of dust, and feeling like somebody ran over my leg with a semi-truck."

He jerked his head, as if physically bringing himself back from bad memories.

"Anyway, I called by other buddy back and asked him what the job was. He met me downtown at a coffee shop—he knew about the drinking so we avoided going to a bar—and told me that there was a man looking for someone to do a little job. I was kind of hesitant at first because my buddy didn't have a lot of details, but when he got to the money I was hooked."

"How much?" Ben asked.

"Ten grand just to watch you and let the man know what you were doing. That's ten grand, five of it up front in cash money, all hundreds."

Ben whistled. He would have taken it too, once upon a time. "So, that much money, you didn't ask a lot of questions, huh?"

Jamie shook his head. "No. Like I told you, I was on a downward slope, man. I needed *something*. So, my buddy gave me a phone, that one I just showed you, and told me the man would be in touch. I wasn't sure if there was anything illegal going on, and I promised myself that if it started looking shady, I would bail. I took the phone and went home.

"The next day a text message showed up asking what kind of car I drove. I had a sweet little Tacoma that I had bought after my first tour in Iraq, but the man on the other end said that was too... what was the word, osten-something..."

"Ostentatious."

"Yeah, that's it. So, I sold it and bought this heap that I'm driving now. I took a picture of it and sent it to ask the man if this would do. He sent back that it was perfect, and gave me information on you with instructions to cruise by your house every once in a while to see what you were up to. I sent him a daily report on your activities. You, uh, you didn't really do a lot the last couple of months."

Ben laughed. No, he hadn't. Retiring from the Army had occupied all his time—turning in equipment, making sure his paperwork was good, all of that. Plus, a yard sale to get rid of all the furniture and crap that he hadn't been able to give away to friends or to Goodwill.

"I cruised by the yard sale but didn't stop," Jamie continued. "Watching you was pretty simple. The man texted me and said that if you ever looked like you were about to leave the area completely to text him immediately and he would let me know what to do. When you got wherever it was you were going, he was going to arrange for me to get the other $5,000."

Jamie stopped and looked at Ben. "Look, man, I don't know you. You don't seem to be a crook or thug or anything like that. Well, except for pulling a gun on me, but I guess I can understand that, kind of had that coming if you knew that I was following you. If I may, I'd like to know what do you do. Who are you for a man I've never met to pay me that much money to keep tabs on you?"

Ben thought for a second. "Didn't you say you thought you heard a name at one point?"

"Yeah. I called my buddy a couple of times, the one who set this all up, and in the background I could have sworn I heard someone say the name Steve or Steven, like that."

Ben rocked back on heels for a second, looked up at the sky. Of course. *That* particular name rang a bell. He ran his hand through his hair, blew out a breath, and looked back at Jamie. Jamie was studying his face, wondering what this was all about. The young man was clearly a little more nervous than he was before.

"That name means something, huh?"

Ben shrugged. "It might. Might be nothing, but I have learned that there are very few true coincidences in this world."

Jamie looked at the ground for a moment, then back at Ben. "So, who *might* this guy be?"

"Let's just leave it at I may know who he is for right now." Ben motioned toward the phone. "I have a plan that requires you taking me on faith that this guy is a real asshole. I am not going to hurt you, I promise you that. But I do need your help because the reason this guy is after me is for something that ain't his. You willing to help?"

"Well…"

"Look. Just tell him the truth, but stretch it a little. That's all. Here's what I want you to tell him."

CHAPTER FOUR

Good Lord in Heaven, why is Customs always such a pain in the ass? Stephen thought. He had nothing to declare, no sir, thank you, thank you for the welcome to the United States. *No, I was in Colombia for business, coffee export and import arrangements. No Cuban cigars, oh goodness, no. Yes, you have a good day too.*

Idiots.

He had turned his phone on as soon as the flight crew had said it was okay upon touching down in Atlanta. Curiously, no messages were waiting.

Stephen walked toward the baggage claim. As he was waiting for his bag to appear, his phoned beeped, indicating a new message.

Subject in Georgia on I-20, traveling west. Will continue to follow and advise.

He grunted to himself. *Is Ben stopping in Mississippi?* Maybe Stephen was close enough to Atlanta to pick up the trail himself. *No, this is why I pay others; let them do it. I'm back in the States now, and Ben is obviously heading toward his old home.*

Stephen made his decision. He collected his bag, went upstairs to the ticket counters, and booked a flight to Memphis, Tennessee.

━┽ ┾━

After the text was sent, Jamie asked, "So…what's the plan?"

Ben thought. If this was *the* Stephen (with a *p*, not a *v*) he thought it might be, he may fall for a ruse. Or maybe not.

"Well, I figure we'll lead him to think that I'm heading to Mexico. If it works, then I won't have to worry about him for a while."

"You think he'll still pay me?" Jamie said, a little anxiously.

Ben doubted it, but said, "Maybe. We'll see how far we can go with it."

Jamie looked at Ben for a solid minute. "Okay, seems to me you know this dude. What's his deal, anyway?"

"That, my friend, is a long story. So. What are you going to do now? If you want, you can continue to follow me. I'm heading to Mississippi, going home. I don't want this Stephen guy knowing exactly what I'm doing because he's trouble. I would explain, but like I said, that's a long damn story and I don't feel like telling it standing here in a field in South Carolina."

Jamie didn't take long to decide. "You appear to think that no matter what you do, he is going to find you eventually, right?"

Ben nodded.

"Well, I've actually met you now, and you don't seem like a bad sort. You mind if I tag along? I have to go *somewhere*. I really don't want to go back to Fayetteville, anyway. There really isn't anything for me there. I still have a good chunk of that $5,000."

"Let me warn you, though, before you make up your mind completely—he is bad news. He paid you for a job, and he doesn't take lightly to anyone messing up a job he has arranged. If you want, play along with him, but I'm asking you to help me with that. You don't have to; I don't have anything close to ten grand to offer you otherwise. I'm asking a huge favor."

"I already made my decision. I know you probably don't have that kind of money, but mister, like I said, I don't have anywhere else to go. This place in Mississippi, you think I could find work there? Solid work instead of being paid to follow people?"

Jamie looked at him, his open face showing honesty. It looked like this boy—*That's what he is*, Ben thought, *just a boy looking for a place in the world*—wanted to do something right in his life. He had thrown in on this job out of desperation because of the money, but didn't seem to Ben the sort who would take to a life on the crooked side.

"Might be. I can't guarantee anything, but I will help you find it if it's there."

"Fair enough. Might be a bad idea but I think I'm going with you. Can't be any worse than the town I grew up in."

Ben grinned. "Just like that, huh? Son, you hardly know me. Hell, not a half hour ago, I had a pistol pointed at your chest."

Jamie smiled a little at that. "You remind me of my old first sergeant. You act like one of those guys who stayed in the Army for twenty years because you liked it, not because you didn't have a lot of options."

Jamie looked at the Blazer, then back at Ben. "You were saying something about not wanting to stand here in this field?"

CHAPTER FIVE

The trip to Mississippi was less than exciting. Ben had to stop a few more times for gas—"I'm pretty sure the Blazer burns gas even when it's turned off," he told Jamie at one stop—and soon they were crossing the state line from Alabama.

Ben always felt odd coming back here. He had grown up in central Mississippi, and every time he had taken leave while in the Army he couldn't wait to get back home where things were familiar. Over the years, though, each time felt a little less magical, as if he were changing but home wasn't. This time, as he drove past the sign welcoming him to the Magnolia State, there was almost no magic at all—a feeling of resignation, maybe a little sadness. The last time he had set foot here was when his mother had passed away almost three years ago.

They drove along Interstate 20 toward Jackson, Ben leading, Jamie behind him in his truck. Ben turned in to a gas station just outside of Meridian to fill up, and Jamie pulled in to the parking lot. He came over as Ben was pumping gas into the Blazer.

"So, this is where you're from, huh?"

Ben looked around. "Not really. We're not too far now, a couple of hours north once we hit I-55. The town I'm from is called Black Creek."

"How far are we from Memphis?"

"About three and a half, four hours. You want to go to Memphis?"

"Yeah, I heard Graceland is pretty awesome. I've never been there."

"One of these days we'll go, then."

Ben turned and looked at Jamie. "Go get that phone out, would you? We need to do something."

Jamie walked back to his car, retrieved the phone, and brought it to Ben.

"Here's what's going to happen. Last text you sent him, you told him I was still headed west on I-20, right?"

Jamie nodded.

"All right then. Send him another one telling him the same thing; you're on my tail as I head toward Louisiana."

Jamie typed out the text, hit *SEND*, and looked at Ben. "Okay, now what?"

"Pull the battery, then break that thing in half."

Jamie hesitated. Ben understood.

"I get it, man—you still don't fully trust me, and I'm telling you to do something that runs against what you were hired to do. All you have is my word that I'm the good guy here, and Stephen is the bad one. All I can promise you is that you don't want to be involved with him—again, my word. You've met me, you ain't met him. He's paid you, I haven't. If you want, you can continue with what you're doing. We're at what you might call a decision point. Your call."

Jamie looked down at the phone in his hand, considering all of this. He looked back at his car, then up at Ben. "Why should I break it, anyway?"

"This guy has been around a while, and I want to make sure he isn't tracking you with one of those apps, you know the ones where if your phone gets stolen or lost you can go find it?"

Jamie nodded, understanding. "You're asking a lot."

"I know I am. Hopefully soon you'll see what kind of man hired you to do this. All I can ask for is your trust."

Jamie continued to look at the phone.

"Fuck it. I'm throwing in with you," he said, then pulled the battery and snapped the flip phone in half.

Ben smiled at him. "Might not be obvious just yet, friend, but you just chose the right side to be on."

⚒ ⚒

Ben finished filling the Blazer with gas and walked over to where Jamie was leaned against his car.

"I need to go on to Black Creek on my own, so when we get around Grenada—about an hour and a half north of here—there's a couple of motels just outside of town. I want you to get a room in one of them and wait until you hear from me."

The nervous look dropped back over Jamie's face. "You don't want me to come with you?"

Ben grinned at him, trying to ease the kid's fears. "Brother, I haven't been home in a while, don't know if anything's changed. I just want to get the lay of the land, do a couple of things I need to get done solo. You've got my number on your cell. Anything looks weird up there, you holler, okay?"

CHAPTER SIX

Black Creek's only claim to fame was that a railroad engineer had lived there for a while back in the 1890s. What set the town apart from others in this part of the world was the fact that there was no town square—since the town really started growing with the expansion of the railroads after the Civil War, Black Creek grew up on both sides of the tracks that ran down the middle of town. There was a historical marker on the north side of town that mentioned something about Union cavalry fighting a skirmish, but the marker was so corroded that it was hard to make out anymore.

The town sat in a slight depression between two low hills, with the creek for which it was named running through it. The two sides of Main Street had once been nothing but saloons, houses of ill repute, and hotels as railroad men, salesmen, and other travelers needed a break from the regular route between Memphis and New Orleans.

Ben signaled to turn onto the road that would shortly become Main Street.

He drove slowly, observing the speed limit, as numerous memories washed over him. He passed the city park on his left, seeing a few people out enjoying the day. April and May are the best months in Mississippi, when the winter has passed and there's a brief respite before it becomes hot and muggy. People had to get out and enjoy it before shutting the doors against the oppressive heat and the mosquitoes that would carry you off somewhere to feast on you at their leisure.

He continued down Main. Two- and three-story buildings, mostly ancient red brick, lined both sides of the street. More of them were occupied than the last time he had been there—it was good to see that downtown was reviving. One business caught his eye—a yoga studio? Here in Black Creek?

He finally saw the place he was looking for and pulled in to a parking slot in front.

Nana's Café had been in the same spot for more than sixty years. Nana herself was long gone, but her daughters and granddaughters continued to serve the best food in town.

Ben walked in, and he was twelve again. He smelled bacon and sausage frying, coffee brewing, and heard every subject under the sun being discussed. He could imagine the finer points of the Reagan Administration being drawn out, as well as what those damn Russians were up to these days. Had things changed? He doubted it. There will always be bad guys and administrations to talk about.

He searched the room, looking for familiar faces. His gaze settled on one person in a uniform. It only took a second to recognize him. Grinning broadly, Ben walked over to the table.

"Hi, Sheriff. Damn dogs are getting into my yard again. Wondering if you could do something about it."

The sheriff had his head down, chewing on a piece of toast as Ben talked. Without looking up, he wiped his mouth with a napkin and grasped the radio microphone that was pinned to his left shoulder.

"Dispatch? Do we have any BOLOs on six-foot-tall white boys, kind of dumb, who don't feel the need to stay in touch with old friends?"

The reply came back. "Um...Sheriff? Say again, please?"

The sheriff grunted, then keyed the microphone again.

"Never mind, dispatch. I'll handle it."

The sheriff looked up. "Well. Look at you. Come to bother me while I'm eating."

Ben was nervous now. "Hey, Reggie, I saw you, thought I'd come over..."

"That what you thought? You thought you could bother the sheriff of Grace County, Mississippi? Thought you could walk in here like you own the place?"

A few other patrons in the café were looking now, and Ben's nervousness grew.

"I'm sorry, man, I haven't been here in a while..."

Reggie's stern face broke into a grin that lit up his features. "Got you, man."

He jumped up and grabbed Ben in a hug. Ben's relief was tremendous as he hugged him back.

They released one another and sat at the table.

"Damn it, man, you completely Lando Calrissian'd me."

"That would make you Han Solo. You ain't cool enough to be Han Solo."

The two looked at each other across the table, old friends taking stock of one another.

"So, where have you been? Haven't seen you since you were here three years ago for your mama's funeral," the sheriff said.

Ben asked the waitress nearby for a cup of black coffee. Turning back to the sheriff, he said, "I was home on emergency leave from Afghanistan, Reggie. I had to go right back."

Reggie nodded. "Kind of figured something like that. You took off in a hurry. I thought you had some place to be."

"Yeah. After that tour was when Lauren finally left, so I just kind of...drifted a while. I finished retiring about two weeks ago."

"Retired, huh? So, are you visiting this time or are you back to stay?"

Ben considered this for a minute. "Don't know yet. Maybe stay, who knows."

Reggie said, "If you want to stay, your mom's house hasn't sold yet. Or if you don't want to be in that house, Linda would put you up in our place. Up to you."

After she placed the cup on the table, Ben thanked the server for his coffee, then took a sip. He leaned back, thinking.

"Don't think on it too much, man. Matter of fact, don't think at all." Reggie looked out the window. "I'm guessing everything you own is in that truck outside, huh?"

Ben nodded.

"It will be fine where it is for right now. Come on, let's go for a ride and catch up. I was just finishing when you walked in." He left money on the table to pay for his meal and Ben's coffee, and the two of them walked out.

⇒‡ ‡⇐

"I was serious about you staying with us if you want," Reggie said as he drove.

"I appreciate it, man. I'm thinking about it."

Reggie drove to the south side of town, then turned onto Highway 34.

"Tell you what. We'll ride out to your mother's place, you can take a look, make up your mind."

"Thanks."

They continued in silence for a couple of minutes, then Reggie said, "All right, what is it? I don't remember you ever being this quiet."

Ben stared straight ahead through the windshield. "Brother, I've been a civilian less than a month. I left Fayetteville with hardly a look back. On the way down here a guy followed me, and I pulled my damn gun on him in a field in South Carolina just off the interstate. You believe that?"

Reggie grunted. "No shit? You didn't shoot him, did you?"

"No. Honestly, the thought never crossed my mind, I just wanted to be ready if he intended me harm, that's all. Ends up he was paid by a man I haven't seen in ten years—dude I only met once, in Afghanistan. That's a long story. Anyway, I talked the guy following me—decent kid named Jamie—into not telling his employer exactly where I was going."

"You must have been pretty persuasive. Oh, that's right—you had a gun on him."

Ben laughed. "Nah, I put it away, man. Kid thought I was going to shoot him in broad daylight right there in that field. I just talked to him, that's all. He seemed to me like someone who wanted somebody else to just listen to what he had to say. I convinced him to tell his employer I was headed for Mexico. All Jamie wanted in return was a job and a place to stay where he could start over."

"That's it?"

"Yeah, he didn't seem really all that into following me anyway. Seemed kind of shady to him, he told me as much. I told him I would help him as much as I could. He's staying in a hotel down in Grenada until I get things settled here."

Reggie thought for a second. "He ain't a criminal, is he? I don't want nobody bringing any trouble into this county. No drugs, no thieving, none of that shit, you hear me?"

"As far as I know, Jamie's on the level. I'll bring him up here, you can meet him. You know anybody who's looking for help?"

"I might. Might be able to help you with that."

CHAPTER SEVEN

Reggie turned off on County Road 1156. The 911 system had mandated that each road have a number for emergency vehicles to find an address. Most folks still referred to the roads by the predominant family that lived in the area, as in "Go down Smith Road past Tom's house, then turn on Cooper Road and you'll find it." When he was growing up here, this road had been Allen Road due to the large farm that belonged to Jerry Allen.

After two miles, Reggie eased the patrol car into a driveway that had two magnolia trees on either side of it. Ben was home.

"Local boy named Scott has been keeping it up," Reggie said. "He cuts the grass, clears off any tree limbs, that sort of thing. If you plan on moving back in here, you'll have to talk to the power and water folks to get your utilities on." He looked at Ben while he spoke, but Ben wasn't paying much attention.

Ben was looking at the sign planted in the front yard that said *FOR SALE*. It depressed him, for some reason—he had never really given much thought to coming back, had even made the arrangements with the realtor to sell the place—but now that he was here, the memories that were faded as he returned started taking on a sharper focus.

Ben appreciated that Reggie kept a respectful distance, not wanting to bother him. Ben would have done the same.

After a few moments, he turned to Reggie.

"Is the inside okay? Do I need to do any repairs on anything?"

Reggie shook his head. "Like I said, Scott's been taking pretty good care of the place. We can go in if you want. There's a key to the back door on top of the door frame."

The two walked around to the rear of the house. As they rounded the back, Ben looked at the woods where the two of them had played as children.

"You remember running around those woods? Fighting Russians like *Red Dawn* or hunting squirrels?"

Reggie laughed. "I do. I also remember running like my head was on fire to get your mom that time you climbed that tree, fell out, and busted your head open."

They both laughed. It hadn't been funny at the time—Ben still had the scar on the back of his head from opening a gash on an exposed tree root after he fell.

"It was your damn fault, Reg. You're the one who dared me to climb as high as I could."

Ben retrieved the key and entered his childhood home.

The young man Scott had done well. The floors were spotless, and although the paint was not fresh, there was a lingering odor that indicated it had not been on the walls for more than a year or so. The house was a little stuffy, so Ben opened a window in the living room and another in the kitchen to get a breeze. The house was filled with the scent of honeysuckle. Ben and his mother had both loved that smell—she had planted several bushes along the side of the house.

He walked to the doorway leading from the kitchen to the living room and ran his hand over the frame. It had not been replaced, only painted over, so he could still imagine the marks made in the wood as he grew. Each year his mother marked his height and praised him for becoming older. Seemed kind of silly to him as a young man—was he accomplishing something by growing? Why be proud of growth? Maybe it's just something mothers do. *Maybe if I had children I could understand.*

He heard the back door close. He figured Reggie had left him to his memories. There were certainly enough of them here, but he was sufficiently tired from driving to be swallowed by them. *Enough of this.* He took another look around, the house completely sterile, no sign of the lives that were lived here. No framed pictures on the wall, no funny cat calendars in the kitchen, no marks on the walls from bumping into them or hitting them with furniture during his mother's numerous attempts to rearrange the look of the house.

This was no longer home. It was just a house now. He chided himself for thinking otherwise. He hadn't had a home in a long time, but now that his time was solely his again and not directed by the Army, maybe that could change.

Could it ever be a *home* again? *His* home? Ben felt a deep desire, a longing, to find a place to set down roots and stay, not thinking about moving ever again. What folks referred to these days as a forever home. The house was just a structure, several walls and a roof. What would make it a home, anyway? A family?

The Army had been his family for a little over twenty years. Whenever he needed shelter, sustenance, a *purpose*—the Army provided. He knew that was what many soldiers told themselves to justify the life, that whatever someone needed would be issued—and signed for. It was an ancient cliché: If you need something, the Army will give it to you.

When the Army isn't around anymore, though…what then?

He closed the windows and locked the door behind him as he left.

CHAPTER EIGHT

The pair rode in silence for a while. The radio squawked a couple of times, but nothing significant enough to warrant Reggie's attention.

Reggie glanced at Ben. Ben had withdrawn into himself, and Reggie saw a faraway look in Ben's eyes that he didn't remember from their time growing up.

"Guess you have a lot on your mind, huh? Was it a bad idea to go to your old house?"

Ben shook his head. "No, brother, it was good to see the place, even as it is. Last time I was there, when Mom was dying, it still looked the way it had when we were kids. Pretty close, anyway. I wasn't really here—I don't know how to explain it properly, but… well, when she passed away, I was home from a rough tour in Afghanistan, you remember. Lots of shit going on in my head."

Reggie thought he understood, but didn't want to press the issue.

"Enough of the heavy stuff, man," Ben said. "It's so good to see you."

Reggie grinned and looked at Ben. "Good to see you too, man. I've missed you."

"I'm taking you up on your offer, at least for tonight. Hope Linda doesn't mind."

"She won't mind at all. She'll be thrilled."

⊷⊹⊶

Later that afternoon, Reggie was returning them to town after touring most of the county. Ben felt good—it had been some time since he had completely relaxed and let someone else drive, for one thing.

The memories of his home continued to come back in focus. They drove past several places where they had shared experiences in their youth—mostly back roads where they had ridden around as teenagers, drinking beer that had been bought by older guys in the neighboring county since it was illegal in their own. That's probably why Reggie was more than likely a good sheriff—he knew where all the hiding places were in Grace County.

As they neared the city limits of Black Creek, Ben asked, "You mentioned something earlier about maybe being able to help me out with that guy who followed me?"

"Yeah. You remember Karen Collins? She was a couple of years behind us in school?"

"Karen? I think so. Why?"

"She has a place out on the east side of town, nice little bar and grill called KC's. You know, after her initials…"

"Yeah, figured that one out, thanks."

"Okay, professor, that's where we're going. When Grace County legalized beer about five years ago, she was the first to open a place to drink. The law had some strings attached—it's still illegal to have a drinking establishment *only*; the place also has to offer food. Same way it's been in Oxford for a while. She took it one step more, man, and this is genius in my humble opinion—any bar must stop serving alcohol at 2:00 AM and midnight on Sunday morning. Look around real quick—you see any Waffle Houses around Black Creek?"

"Uh…no…"

"And Nana's doesn't open until 7:00. What's a poor drunk to do from 2:00 to 7:00 if he's hungry? Hungry and drunk? Karen took care of that. At 2:00 AM, the grill is open, serving up eggs, waffles, bacon, all that until 5:00. Gives folks a chance to sober up a little, keeps them off the roads, and she's making a killing.

"I love it," Reggie went on. "I still send a deputy out there occasionally, but I always hear the next day that everybody was well behaved, sitting there eating breakfast and drinking coffee until she has to kick them out. Even the bad drunks, and we have a couple. Since she opened her doors, DUIs in this county have gone down."

"Good for her. What's this got to do with me?"

Reggie smiled. "All that business requires some dedication, brother. She needs help, and the last two or three ain't worked out too well. You say this fellow Jamie needs work in a bad way? He can prove to me that he's as decent as you say *plus* get himself a good start if Karen agrees to take him on. Ain't going to lie—she'll work his ass into the ground."

KC's was a one-story wooden building with a porch running along the front. It looked like an old-time country grocery store. As they pulled into the gravel parking lot, Ben remarked as much and Reggie pointed out the two slight humps in the gravel where the gas pumps had once been in front.

It was ten minutes to 7:00 when they arrived, and there were several pickups and cars already there.

"Pretty busy. Guess she has good food, huh?"

"Yeah. Nana's closes at 6:00, and unless you want Mexican food or a cheeseburger for supper, this is the only place to go nearby. The food is good, though—she got a good chef, guy who came down from Memphis a couple of years back. He fell in love with the town, decided to stay, and now makes a pretty good steak."

They walked in.

The bar ran the length of the restaurant down the left side. There were booths on the right, and tables in the middle. Reggie guided Ben toward the booths, and they took a seat. The place was half full, and more cars had been pulling in after them.

There was a large mirror behind the bar. The usual bar signs—liquor license, *NO UNDER 21 ALLOWED AFTER 9:00 PM, CHILDREN LEFT UNATTENDED WILL BE PUT TO WORK*—were all attached to it, along with a single dollar bill. Along the top of the mirror was a string of Christmas lights. Ben always felt that a proper watering hole should have these lights up year-round. He couldn't explain why.

"Don't have to wait for a hostess to seat you, huh? My kind of place," Ben said.

"Oh, there's times when folks have to wait. There's picnic tables out back for when the weather's nice. That's where everybody who smokes goes to eat, so they're usually full." Reggie slid into the booth. He picked up a menu and handed it to Ben. "The pulled pork is awesome, highly recommend it. Don't even need sauce—they smoke it every day out back."

That sounded good to Ben. He looked around, noticed a few faces that looked familiar—even a couple that had been in Nana's earlier that day when he first walked up to Reggie's table.

"Everybody looks like they're eyeballing me."

Reggie laughed. "It isn't *that* unusual for me to have supper with someone new in town, or someone who hasn't been here in a long time, in your case—but folks still get a little curious. You grew up here, you know what I'm talking about."

"I do indeed."

The server brought their meals. Ben had a beer, while Reggie drank sweet tea—"Still officially on duty, I guess," he said—and once they cleared their plates, Ben said, "Doesn't Linda get mad if you don't eat at home? I don't want to cause any trouble for you."

Reggie laughed. "No, man, it isn't trouble. Most days I get home too late for supper, and she ends up working 'til all hours up at the university anyway. Theresa is old enough now to where we don't have to be home all the time. It'll be all right—well, until it ain't. You know how that goes."

Ben agreed. He hadn't been married to Lauren very long, but he fully understood how things were okay until they weren't.

"Before we take off, I want you to talk to Karen. Look—here she comes now. She usually comes over when I come in to eat."

Ben turned and saw a woman in her thirties walking out from the kitchen. He tried to amend his memories of her in high school to fit what he saw now—a girl who had never been what he and his friends called "fine" or "hot"—"fine" being the term most commonly used when he was in school—who was now strikingly beautiful. Dark blonde hair pulled back in a ponytail, blue eyes that seemed to sparkle twenty years ago but now, probably due to running a business, had a serious set to them. Ben saw a figure that was more athletic than he remembered, even in faded Levi's and a dark blue shirt.

Karen saw the two of them and smiled when she saw Reggie. She glanced at Ben, and he saw some recognition in her eyes.

As she walked over, she said "Sheriff, good to see you. Sara told me you were in here with some stranger. Did y'all enjoy the pork?"

"Sure did. Karen, you remember Ben?"

Karen held out her hand to Ben and said, "Sure do. It's been a while, though. How are you?"

Ben took her hand, held it for probably a second or two longer than he should have, then let go. "I'm good. Looks like you're doing pretty well for yourself. I like the place."

She beamed. "Thanks. I'm trying hard. Sheriff, scoot over. I've got a couple of minutes before it starts getting too crazy in here."

Reggie moved over to give her room, and she sat in the booth directly across from Ben.

"I was really sorry about your mother, Ben. She was a good woman. I didn't get a chance to talk to you when you were here for her funeral."

"Thank you. I had to get back, didn't get a chance to talk to everybody I wanted to."

"I understand. Which one—Iraq or Afghanistan?"

"Afghanistan. How'd you know about that?"

She laughed. "Come on, you haven't been gone that long, have you? One, this is a small town; everybody knows everybody else's business. Two, your mother was one of my first steady customers when I opened KC's, before the sickness took her. We'd talk about you all the time."

"I don't remember her mentioning you, I mean, I remember *you*, but she never talked about you."

Her smile drew back slightly. "I know. She told me she didn't talk about me to you, and I didn't mind too much. I knew you and your wife were having problems, and she thought it was...well, a little indecent to talk about another woman to you. That was *her* word, not mine, by the way. She was something special.

"I helped her set up her email, and she both loved it and hated it when you would send her pictures of yourself somewhere, all bearded up with a rifle, and in the email you would say, 'Can't tell you where I am, but here I am, proof that I'm still alive.'"

Ben suddenly felt terrible. After the situation with Lauren began to deteriorate, he emailed his mother more often. *How could I burden her with my own bullshit when she obviously had her own problems?*

Karen noticed the change in expression on his face. "Hey—I just met you again after a long time, and I'm running off at the mouth." She turned to Reggie. "Everything going okay in the wilds of Grace County, Mr. Lawman?"

"As far as you know."

She laughed again. Ben thought he could listen to that laugh for the rest of his life and never get tired of it. *Careful, though*, he thought—didn't he feel the same way about his ex wife at one point?

"So…Mama came in here a lot, huh?"

Karen turned back to Ben. "Yes, she did. I loved that woman; she was so funny! After she was bedridden, I'd go over and see her whenever I could."

Ben didn't know what to say. His mother had mentioned a couple of times about someone who was looking after her besides the nurse, but had never offered details. At that point, Ben was so wrapped up in his deployment and his dissolving marriage that it never occurred to him to ask.

"Thank you so much. I don't know how I could ever repay you."

Reggie spoke up. "I think I might."

Karen turned to Reggie, eyebrows raised. "Really?"

Reggie gestured to Ben. "He just got back into town this morning, but he may have a line on someone who can help you out around here. Go on, tell her about that guy."

She looked at Ben expectantly.

"Well, Reg was telling me you've been having some trouble with your employees."

Karen nodded.

"I brought a guy with me from North Carolina. How he came to travel with me is another story, but I think he might be a good fit in here."

She considered for a moment. "Is he over twenty-one? I could really use somebody behind the bar, give me a break so I'm not always back there."

"Yes, he is. He was medically discharged after getting shot in Afghanistan, and he's looking for work. He seems to be eager to get on with his life somewhere, and I told him where I was going."

"You trust him?"

"I haven't gotten to know his whole life story or anything, but yeah, for some reason I do. I'll tell you everything about him that I know, if you want. He's from Texas, if that helps any."

"I'll think about it. Bring him in sometime." She looked around. Several customers were now standing, waiting on tables as the room had filled up.

"Gotta go, boys. Sheriff, always good to see you. Ben...don't be a stranger, okay? Come on in anytime."

Ben watched as she walked back to the kitchen. Reggie noticed this, and leered at Ben. "Noticed the view, I see?"

Ben felt the blush go all the way into his scalp. "What are we, fifteen again?"

Reggie laughed. "She's something, ain't she?"

"Yes, she is."

⋇ ⋇

Reggie drove Ben back to his Blazer, still parked outside Nana's.

"Good to see I didn't get a parking ticket."

"I let the city boys know to leave it alone, man, a war hero was back in town."

"Fuck you," Ben said as he got out of the patrol car. He leaned in the passenger window and asked, "I'm just following you, right?"

"Yeah. I'm going to call home, let Linda know I'm on my way. I'm not going to tell her about you; I want it to be a surprise."

⋇ ⋇

They pulled in front of Reggie's house. It was a two-story Victorian that Reggie and Linda had bought several years before, when he moved back to Black Creek. The country around was quiet, and was the main attraction for him when he and his new wife made

39

the decision—both wanted a place to raise a family, but more importantly after Memphis, they wanted peace and quiet.

An American flag jutted from one of the columns on the front porch, and the air was sweet with the smell of jasmine and roses. The house was well cared for, and Ben felt at home as soon as he got out of his truck. This is the way things should be.

Reggie walked around past a dark green Civic parked next to the garage. The Civic had a university staff sticker on the windshield, and Ben surmised it must be Linda's car.

"She's home; be quiet when we go in," Reggie instructed.

They walked up the brick steps and through the door.

CHAPTER NINE

"Hey baby! Where you at?" Reggie called.

"In the kitchen" came the response.

Reggie grinned as he held a finger to his lips. He moved through the foyer into the living room. "Honey, I found a stray white boy wandering around, can I keep him?"

"What are you—" Linda started, then saw Ben. She jumped up and ran to him from the kitchen table. "Benjamin Martin! What on earth are you *doing* here?"

Ben hugged her as she came close. He thought she was going to break a rib if she didn't stop.

As he withdrew from her embrace, he looked her up and down. "Still just as pretty as ever, Linda."

"You aren't looking too bad yourself. Come on in the kitchen." She swatted at Reggie. "Why didn't you tell me he was back?"

"I wanted to surprise you, honey. Can he stay?" Reggie whined.

Linda laughed. "I suppose. You know how I feel about taking in strays. As long as he doesn't mess on the carpet."

Linda had gone to bed, begging off early as she told them she had to be up and at work early the next morning. She admonished them not to make a mess, and told Ben he could stay as long as he liked.

Ben and Reggie walked out on the back porch and sat in rocking chairs, each with a beer in their hands.

"You don't have to work tomorrow?" Ben asked.

"I'm taking a personal day. Told the deputies to give me a call, anything they can't handle on their own. Besides, today's Thursday and I told them I'd work the weekend—Linda's got papers to grade and Theresa is going somewhere with the church group. House was going to be empty anyway—well, I needed to vacate because Linda hates any noise when she's working in the house." He took a long pull from his beer.

"Talk to me, man. How have you been?"

Ben hesitated. How much was he willing to discuss? There was so much, and even though Reggie was his dearest, oldest friend, there were still things that a civilian just couldn't understand. Ben swallowed half of the beer in his bottle and started talking.

"That last time I was home, for Mama's funeral. There was a drawdown going on in Afghanistan, Iraq was done, but our mission load was still heavy and I felt a lot of damn guilt over coming home. Everybody told me, 'Don't worry, it's your *mother* for Christ's sake, go take care of everything. We'll be fine, the Army and the war will still be here when you get back.' While I was here taking care of the funeral arrangements, I was watching the television at the funeral home while I was waiting to sign some paperwork. News from Afghanistan had taken on a 'Ho hum, there was an incident, two US soldiers or Marines are dead, next up is weather in your area,' that kind of shit. There was some footage of the attack, a God Almighty big bomb going off in Kabul. They had released the names of the two guys killed and had their pictures on the screen. I was just with those guys two weeks before, and if I hadn't come home on leave I probably would have been one of the casualties."

"Jesus."

"Yeah. So, I was freaked out about it—on one hand glad I was still alive and the other hand asking myself why I wasn't there. Dumb, right? I've read about survivor's guilt, and the real pain comes from the two sides fighting it out in your head—guilt. Heavy ass guilt. I'm happy to be still drawing air on this side of the ground, and I feel like a piece of shit for feeling that way. Why them, and why not me? Nobody blames me for coming home for a funeral, but *I was supposed to be there.* One of the guys killed was my assistant team sergeant. He took over after I got the Red Cross message to come back to Black Creek because my mother was dying. They had gone to Kabul just to get a briefing for a mission coming up. I play the what-if game all the time. What if, what if, what if. What if this, what if that? It's stupid, but I can't stop."

It had all come out in a burst. Ben felt a little better.

"Don't do it man, you'll burn yourself out. I was never in the military, but something similar happened when I was on the force in Memphis."

Ben looked at Reggie. "You never told me about anything like that."

"It was a long time ago, when I first got hired on. I was a rookie, and this was before they mandated that all officers wear vests, back in the late '90s. I was out with my partner, an old-school cop if there ever was one. He hated the vests, and didn't wear one. The ones we had back then were uncomfortable as hell, and you pretty much lost five pounds in sweat during every shift. Thing is, he also believed that presence was the best tool every law enforcement officer has, and if we roll out like we're going to downtown Baghdad, well, how is the public going to respect that?

"We responded to a call, couple of thugs roughing up a girl in south Memphis. We got there, were calming everybody down, getting tempers cooled off. The girl was in bad shape, and a crowd had gathered. The two thugs weren't from that neighborhood, so everyone there was yelling for us to get that trash off the streets.

"We were putting the cuffs on them when the girl's brother came around the corner with a pistol, shooting away, trying to kill the two idiots who were beating on his sister. I don't know if he was high or just pissed off, but he was intent on getting them.

"The first round hit one of the thugs behind his left ear and came out his right eye. I was frozen in place, man, couldn't move. I had my hand on his head putting him in the car when I heard a *snap* right next to me, then a *thunk*. It sounded like somebody dropping a watermelon on the pavement. I had his blood all over me, and I just stared at his head. It was surreal.

"My partner, being the veteran police officer that he was, pushed the other one to the ground and drew his weapon as he dropped to one knee to return fire and protect the guy. The girl's brother either didn't notice or didn't care that he was now shooting at a cop; all he wanted was to kill the other thug. Three rounds hit my partner in the chest, with a fourth blowing out his carotid artery. He was dead in seconds—nothing I could do but stand there like an idiot. I saw my partner go down and finally came to my senses. I drew my own weapon and put the brother down with two shots while he was *still* banging away at the thug on the ground. Got a medal for it. You believe that?"

Ben could absolutely believe that.

"Shit happens to everyone, especially in the lines of work we have chosen. Now, I haven't had to shoot anyone since. I consider myself very fortunate for that fact. Thing is, I don't *want* to have to shoot anybody. I feel that my duty as a peace officer is not to only enforce the *law* but also the *peace*. That's a feeling that most lawmen have...it just doesn't play too well on TV so nobody much hears about it."

Ben nodded. "I know, man. Hell, I was in intelligence, I never even *expected* to have to kill anybody. But it happens sometimes."

"You feel guilty about that?"

"What? Guilty about putting some jackass who's trying to kill me and my friends in the ground? Absolutely not."

"Yeah, you say that, but it doesn't sound like you mean it."

"Look. I ain't a killer, I ain't a murderer. I was in combat, and the three times I actually *saw* the motherfucker trying to kill me, I didn't think, I didn't hesitate. I lined up my sights and pulled the trigger. That's it. Out of five tours totaling a little over three and a half years of my life, I know for a fact that I killed three men by my lonesome; the rest was either twenty dudes all banging away at the enemy or indirect fire blowing them straight to hell. Airplanes, artillery, heavy weapons, all that—that was the reality of combat for me in Afghanistan, most of the time you never even saw them, you just shot back at where their fire was coming from."

Reggie didn't say anything, was content to let his friend get it out.

Ben looked down and realized he was squeezing his beer as he talked. He willed himself to relax, allowing blood to return to his white knuckles.

He sighed. "Okay brother, I didn't want to talk to you and cry on your shoulder about my tours. What I have to talk to you about does concern Afghanistan, though."

Ben reached in his pocket, retrieved a small object, and tossed it on the table between them.

Reggie picked it up. Plastic, about two inches long and less than an inch wide. It was a light green, the same shade that used to be in hospitals. It looked like it had four posts coming out of the bottom of it at some time, but three had snapped off. On the top, along one edge was what looked like a representation of a rifle cartridge.

"You know, except for being so thick on the bottom, this looks like a follower in a rifle magazine."

"That's exactly what it is. If you push against the bottom of it where you see the seam, you'll find a USB memory stick."

Reggie did as Ben said, and soon the familiar USB connection was exposed.

"Huh. Why would someone go to the trouble of putting a drive in one of these?"

"That is a long story."

CHAPTER TEN

BAGRAM AIR FIELD, AFGHANISTAN - JUNE 2005

The United States military, wherever it goes in the world, follows a pattern when it comes to providing a place for people to live. First, there are tents—gigantic canvas and plastic structures that are drafty and almost always smell terrible. When it is decided that a more permanent place is needed because they are going to be there for a while, the next step is the B-hut, short for barracks hut. An open bay plywood building, they are also drafty and smell terrible. Eventually, as in Afghanistan, concrete buildings are constructed, but one can always find the B-huts.

The door to the B-hut opened slowly, letting the Afghan sunlight in. The heavy fall of boots sounded on the plywood floor as the shadow moved from bunk to bunk. Ben was awake as soon as the door opened, but hoped that he was not the intended target.

Tough luck. The shadow moved near his cot.

"Sergeant Martin? Is Sergeant Martin in here?"

A few responses, mostly "Shut the goddamn door" and "Fuck off" came back. The shadow looked around.

Ben raised his head. "What?"

"You awake?" the shadow asked, unnecessarily. "You got a message, somebody wants to talk to you."

Ben struggled to open his eyes. Sleep was just too rare in this place, and he enjoyed his. He rubbed his face and looked up.

"Who from?" he croaked.

"Don't know; they want you in the TOC." The shadow turned and let the door slam behind him as he left.

Ben rolled onto his side and put his feet on the floor. He sat for a minute, staring at nothing, then sighed and pulled his boots on.

The Tactical Operations Center (TOC) in Bagram looked like every other operations center that Ben had ever been in. The movies always portray these centers as high-tech areas where everyone is focused on their computer screens, large LCD television sets on the walls, clean cut individuals with headsets relaying information to their supervisors in hushed tones.

Reality is a little different. The plywood walls barely keep the omnipresent dust from coating everything. As Ben entered, one soldier argued with another about *Battlestar Galactica* while another played solitaire on his computer. Energy drink cans or coffee cups were at every position. The desks were three long plywood tables with computers spaced about a foot apart, with cables running to each in bundles. On the main wall facing the desks were several large screens, showing the day's missions as well as any available live feeds from the battlefield. Each table was slightly lower than the one behind it, making the room seem like an amphitheater. At the back of the tables was a shorter desk where the battle captain and the operations sergeant major sat to observe and control the activities. The battle captain was a rotating duty between officers, most of the time during daytime being the commander.

The operations sergeant major was reading something on his computer as he sipped coffee from a Styrofoam cup.

"Sergeant Major, do you know who wants to see me? I heard I have a message."

The man looked up from his desk. "Hey. Martin. Good. Let's take a walk."

The two walked out of the TOC and into the hallway. The sergeant major turned to Ben. "Let's go outside. You still smoke?"

"Every once in a while, Sergeant Major."

"Okay. I need one while I talk to you about this."

Somewhere in every United States military compound is an empty fifty-gallon drum that is used to burn sensitive documents. This is so they don't pile up after they are no longer needed; there is no shredder. Coincidentally, it is usually located near a smoking area, and this one was to the rear of the operations center building. Two soldiers stood near the barrel, and when they saw the sergeant major approaching with someone, it occurred to them that there was somewhere else they needed to be. In seconds, Ben and the sergeant major were alone.

"Take a seat, Sergeant Martin."

Ben swung his legs through to sit at the picnic table near the burn barrel. Picnic tables—another omnipresent thing in American military camps. Ben opened the pocket on his sleeve and pulled a pack of cigarettes out. He offered one to the sergeant major.

"No thanks, got my own," he said as he retrieved his and lit one.

"Okay, Martin, I remember you supporting my guys a couple of years back when I was a team sergeant. We were down around Kandahar."

"I remember that, Sergeant Major. Was that when Reilly got hit?" Ben said, referring to the team's medic.

"Yeah. He ended up doing okay, but he was medically retired after that."

Ben nodded. He had been in the Humvee next to the one Reilly was in.

The sergeant major shook his head, as if to rid himself of the memory and get back to matters at hand. "Only reason I bring it up is because I know you, and how you perform under fire. I've had support guys freak out when the going gets tough. Hell, I hate to admit it but I've seen SF guys get a little freaked out too. Shit happens. But I think you know that I do give a shit about all my soldiers, tabbed or not. You understand?"

Ben nodded again, wondering where this was going.

"Okay." The sergeant major exhaled forcefully, preparing himself. "What I want to know is, do you have any idea—any idea *whatsoever*—why you are being ordered to go on a mission that is coming straight from OGA? Something that whenever the commander or I ask for details, we are told to mind our own damn business and just get it done?"

Ben's face showed a fair amount of surprise. OGA could mean anyone—the letters stood for Other Government Agency, and usually referred to the Central Intelligence Agency but could be anyone from the NSA to the State Department.

"I have no idea. I just came back here to Bagram to get new radio fills for the next month and turn in receipts for the operations fund we've used. Last I heard, we were going on another mission starting in three days."

The sergeant major nodded. "Well, that mission is scratched. The team you were with is on standby and you are going straight to Orgun-E to meet up with an OGA guy for something I'm not allowed to know about."

"Sergeant Major, I'm telling you, I don't know anything about this."

The sergeant major gave him a hard stare. "Look. This theater has kind of taken a back seat because of Iraq. All the assets we have are given priority over there and we're getting the leftovers. What we have, we must use wisely. This mission—whatever it is—is taking my soldiers away from the job we have to do. If it's something worthwhile, then so be it. What chaps my ass is being told to shut up and color, you get me?"

"I do. Again, I have no clue. Why the hell OGA wants me specifically is beyond me. I've helped them out before, but I've never been requested by name."

Both men stopped talking as two F-15s spun their engines up for takeoff. The runway was less than a quarter mile away, and the jet noise made talking impossible until the planes were airborne. They watched the aircrafts lift off and climb over the mountains.

The sergeant major turned to Ben once the noise died. "Okay, Martin. Go to the S-3 Air section; there's a bird leaving in an hour going straight to Orgun-E. Get on it. When you arrive, Captain Rodriguez's team will meet you at the airfield and they will escort you to your next destination, which I am also not privy to."

Ben rose from the table. "Roger, Sergeant Major."

The sergeant major's face softened a little. "I'm not pissed at *you*, Martin. I have a good idea none of this is your doing. When you get done, if you can, I'd like to know what happened so at least I can be aware. I've never trusted these OGA guys. I've worked with them on several occasions. It rarely seems to work out to our benefit. We're *supposed* to be on the same side, but I wonder sometimes."

"I will let you know whatever I can, Sergeant Major. Thanks."

The sergeant major nodded, finished his cigarette, and went back inside.

CHAPTER ELEVEN

The Chinook helicopter is a marvel of engineering. With two giant rotors turning in opposite directions, the entire airframe shimmies and shakes as if it's just waiting for the right moment to completely fall apart. To say it is noisy on the inside is a massive understatement. There's a common saying in the Army—helicopters are just 6,000 parts flying in close formation.

Ben was sitting in the rearmost seat on the left side. The seats were nylon webbing strapped across aluminum tubing that he was sure the Army designed to make it uncomfortable to the point that you had no problem wanting to get the hell off the aircraft when the time came. The rear gate of the helicopter was open, with a gunner seated behind a machine gun pointing out to cover the area behind them.

The view out the back was fascinating to Ben. Funny thing—Afghanistan didn't look too bad from up here. Mountains thrust up from the desert floor, valleys that were a deep green, the occasional village filled with herds of goats and sheep. Ben had the feeling that, except for the Toyota trucks he could see on the roads, this is what life looked like a thousand years ago.

Ben felt the helicopter begin to descend and knew they were close.

＝┼┼＝

There was a large sign next to the helicopter landing area that said *WELCOME TO ROCKET CITY.* Ben had been through Orgun-E before; the mountains that surrounded the American base gave perfect observation to the activities there, plus there was the added benefit of being able to launch 107mm rockets with little chance of being discovered. Two full sections of US Army artillery stationed there returned fire when the rockets were coming in, but the regularity of the fire from the mountains revealed that the American artillery wasn't often effective enough.

There was a Humvee waiting at the edge of the landing area. Ben was the only passenger, but there were four large orange nylon bags marked *MAIL* that came on the helicopter with him. Two soldiers ran up and grabbed the bags after Ben stepped off the bird. Another soldier approached, fully bearded and looking annoyed.

"You Martin?" he asked.

"That's me," Ben replied.

"Okay, grab your shit and follow me."

＝┼┼＝

The Special Forces compound was attached to the main American base, with its own gate and Afghan guards. One of the Afghans opened the gate so Ben and the soldier could drive through. The soldier hadn't said a word since he picked Ben up, and now it was

Ben's turn to be annoyed. After they drove through the gate, Ben turned to him and asked, "Where is Captain Rodriguez?"

Without turning to look at him, the soldier replied, "You'll meet him in a couple of minutes. He's *really* looking forward to meeting you. Your buddy is already here, talking to the captain right now."

Buddy? Ben thought. *This should be good.*

The soldier dropped Ben off in front of a small concrete building, and after Ben had collected his gear, the soldier drove off without a word. Ben looked at the top of the building, saw all the antennas and surmised that this must be the operations center. He pulled open the wooden door that was held shut by a plastic water bottle filled with dirt attached to parachute cord running over a nail at the top of the frame. As he walked in, the weight of the bottle pulled the door shut behind him.

Inside were three men, one of whom had a radio handset pressed to his ear as he wrote something on a pad of paper. The other two were huddled around a laptop, discussing something on the screen. When the door opened and they saw Ben, the two at the laptop looked up. One of them, a Hispanic man, motioned Ben to come over.

"You Martin?" he asked.

Does anyone do anything but grunt and ask simple questions here?

"That's me," Ben replied, feeling a little déjà vu.

"Come on over. I'm Captain Rodriguez; my team will be running this show."

The way he said it led Ben to think the captain was daring him to say otherwise.

"This is Stephen, the OGA representative for this little outing we're going on."

Ben held out his hand to Stephen and sized him up. Late forties, early fifties, dressed in the typical civilian government worker/government contractor outfit—cargo pants (khaki, of course), button-up shirt with pockets everywhere (also khaki, of course), and a baseball cap with a piece of Velcro on the front for attaching cool guy patches. The state of his clothes said he bought them yesterday. Tactical sunglasses had been placed on the front of his ball cap.

Stephen took his hand and shook it, also sizing Ben up. There was a fleeting look of recognition in his eyes, like he'd seen Ben before. "Stephen Dawson. Nice to meet you finally. You're the one who is responsible for all of this, I hear."

The captain grunted. "Yeah, I love nothing more than hearing, 'Drop what you're doing, here's a new mission for you that we can tell you nothing about.'"

Stephen smiled. Ben thought he had never seen condescension more evident in a facial expression. He turned to face Captain Rodriguez.

"Yes, Captain, it is true there is a lot of secrecy in this mission. There must be. If I could tell you more, I would."

Bullshit, Ben thought. *You are definitely the type of guy who enjoys knowing something others aren't allowed to know.*

Ben was trying to figure out exactly why he had taken an immediate dislike to this man. Maybe because he seemed out of sorts in this place, just uncomfortable being out here in the dirt where the war was. Stephen seemed to eye everything around him with distaste, as if he were above this sort of thing. Ben wondered what was so important that it dragged Stephen away from whatever it was that he normally did.

The captain looked down at the laptop, then back up at Ben.

"Guess you're ready for this, Sergeant. I hope all of this is worth it, whatever it is you're supposed to do."

Ben was getting angry. "Look sir, I just got told about this shit *this morning*. I'm supposed to be supporting operations going on out west, supporting another team. I flew to Bagram just to pick up some supplies. Next thing I know, the sergeant major is telling me to get my ass down here for something even *he* doesn't know about. You can stand there and be pissed all you want, but I just want you to know I'm in the goddamned dark as much as *you* are. *Sir.*"

The captain was taken aback, and it showed on his face. Great thing about being in the Special Operations field, a non-commissioned officer is allowed (unofficially, of course) to speak his mind to an officer without serious repercussions. Not always, but due to the small size of the units in the field, everyone is allowed a little leeway. Serious disrespect is one thing and is not tolerated, but speaking your mind when things start to look dangerous is encouraged.

"You really don't know anything about this, huh?" the captain said, softening a bit in his tone.

"No sir, I don't."

"All right. And you've never met Stephen before?"

"First time."

The captain nodded. Ben could tell the two of them were on the same page regarding Stephen, and he relaxed.

"Fine, Martin. Allow me to show you why this has me pissed."

He spun the laptop around, and Ben was looking at a map of the area.

"Good news—we will have air cover as we move, convoy style, to this area." He indicated a spot on the map to the east, on the border of Afghanistan and Pakistan. "We'll have four gun trucks, plus four Afghan National Army Hilux trucks, as we move through here." He drew a vertical line with his finger from their current location east to the area on the border.

"We only have air cover for the duration of the movement. There will be two A-10s overhead in case anything goes to hell. This pass"—he pointed again to the area between the two locations—"is the Mane Kandow pass, where that ranger was killed last year."

Ben nodded. He had been through the area once before, when the firebase was established on the border.

"Our destination is this little outpost named for the area— Lwara. Once we get there tomorrow evening, we'll remain overnight until the next morning, when you'll be going on your mission."

Ben asked, "Any reason we can't fly out there?"

The captain grimaced. "There aren't enough aircraft right now. What is in country has been moved out west for that operation you were supposed to be on. Everything else, including all the damn air support, has been shifted to Iraq for the time being. What we got is what we got. Besides, I've been told the boys out at Lwara need some help with some shit they have going on, so they'll appreciate some additional gun trucks."

"Shit. That's all the good news?"

The captain laughed. "Oh, we're just getting to the bad news. When you're doing, well, *whatever* it is you're doing, there will be no eyes in the sky, no air support, *nada*."

"No ISR at all?" Ben asked, referring to Intelligence, Surveillance, and Reconnaissance platforms. Typically unmanned aircraft, like Predator drones, that were outfitted with cameras and other sensors to allow everyone on the ground to know what was happening in their area.

"Nope. Other bad news—satellites have been re-tasked for Iraq as well, so no overhead either. We're going in blind and deaf. Well"—he paused—"*you* are. Once we get to the border we are stopping. We can't cross over to provide you any support. My mission is to get you there alive, and once you cross the border, *if* you come back, to bring you back here."

Ben looked at Stephen, who had been quiet this entire time.

"So, are you the guy who knows what it is I'm supposed to do?"

Stephen leaned forward from the table. He flashed a smile.

"Honestly, I also don't know exactly. All I know, which is just a little more than the captain here, is that we are to get you across the border to meet with someone who has information we want."

Ben frowned. "That's it? Information? Really? So why the hell am I involved?"

Stephen maintained the smile, which Ben suddenly felt the urge to put his fist in.

"Thing is, my friend, is that the source of the information requested you by name. As in Martin, Benjamin, Staff Sergeant, US Army."

Ben contemplated this for a second. "By name, huh? Didn't know I was that famous."

"The channels that the request followed have been used in the past for serious intelligence regarding terrorist movements and plans for a while now, even back before September 11. The source is highly reliable, vouched for by people who are vetted. The intelligence has always been solid. Came in like clockwork, made our job easy.

"Then, six months ago, nothing. Not a peep. We had assets all over the world scrambling, trying to figure out what happened to this source, but no one could find him. If it *is* a him. We still don't know."

Ben said, "No idea who this guy or gal is, huh?"

The smile dropped off Stephen's face in an instant, as if he were tired of using those muscles.

"I have my suspicions, but no solid information. Three days ago, a message from the source asked for you specifically to come to a certain location. The source has information, but will only divulge it to *you*. Believe me," he said, sweeping his hand around the tiny room in a grand gesture, "if the source wasn't so valuable, none of this would be happening right now."

I have been involved in some weird situations, Ben thought, *but this has got to be the weirdest. What the hell does this have to do with me?*

The captain spoke up. "That's it, my man. Short notice, I know. Go get ready, grab some chow if you want. We're stepping off toward Lwara in an hour."

"Which truck am I in?" Ben asked, walking with the captain toward the vehicles lined up in front of the gate.

"You will be in mine, and Stephen in the team sergeant's truck. Rear seat, passenger side, right behind me so I can keep an eye on you."

Ben opened the door to the first Humvee and threw in his gear. After putting on his body armor, he checked his rifle to ensure there was a full magazine in it. He then waited for the trip to begin, trying to process all that was happening.

━━◁┼ ┼▷━━

Stephen walked toward the last Humvee in the line and put his bag in the truck's rear driver's side seat. He had body armor as well, just not with so many pouches as the rest of these Neanderthals. *Really,* he thought, *look at them—every one of them with bushy beards, Oakley sunglasses, and enough armament to take down a city. Jesus, one of them even has a sawed off double-barreled shotgun strapped on his back. What the hell does one need something like that for?*

He walked over to the team sergeant, an older man who was poring over the map of their destination. "One thing I've wanted to ask—why does everyone grow beards?"

The team sergeant looked up, clearly annoyed that this guy was asking dumbass questions right as they were getting ready to leave.

"Main reason is, Afghans don't really respect a man that can't grow facial hair. Other reason is, even though we're not Afghans, at a distance dudes with beards all generally look alike, so the Taliban hesitate to shoot right at us all the time in case one of us turns out to be a fellow Muslim. See, if a bullet from their rifle kills a Muslim, then that must be Allah's will, not the asshole pulling the trigger intending to kill a brother. Understand?"

The team sergeant turned back to his map.

━━◁┼ ┼▷━━

"I got to tell you, I wasn't too excited about you showing up," the captain said to Ben. "This knucklehead Stephen got here last night, walked in like he owned the damn place and started barking orders. When I was getting ready to throw him out on his ass, a message came down from headquarters saying to give this dude every courtesy, cooperation to the fullest, and another individual would be arriving today on the mail bird."

They were standing next to the captain's Humvee, which was now running. He leaned in to the passenger's side, grabbed the hand mic for the radio, and responded to a radio check from the other vehicles.

"I figured you would be another OGA shitbird. Guess not."

"Nope. Just a regular guy."

The captain grunted. "I doubt that. At least you're in our unit, that's something. I've worked with these dudes before. I've known some good ones, too. One of my friends I went to college with back in Miami ended up going the OGA route a couple of years back. I ran into him in Jalalabad on my last tour. 'Course, he doesn't have the same attitude this Stephen does."

"C'mon, sir, there's assholes in every organization. This guy just seems to be a higher-ranking asshole than usual."

"Yeah. All right, let's get this show on the road."

The vehicles left the gate in a single column, two Afghan trucks leading the way, four Humvees in the middle, and the other two Afghan trucks bringing up the rear. After test firing their weapons outside the base, the convoy started up the hill leading toward the Mane Kandow pass.

Ben heard over the radio that the A-10s were on station. He felt comforted that this particular type of airplane was overhead, ready to rain down destruction should the need arise. He was slightly surprised that a short notice mission like this one was able to justify having them. He had heard that the Air Force hated the things—the aircraft had been designed back in the 1970s to destroy Soviet tanks and can keep flying with half of the plane shot away, and the Air Force thought they were ugly as hell—they aren't *fighter jets.* Not sexy enough, and they were designed to support *ground troops.* God forbid people on the ground need help.

Of course, ground guys loved them. The plane was built around a 30mm Gatling gun, and in his last two tours Ben had had the pleasure of hearing the *brrrt* sound they made when they engaged a target. Usually there was nothing left of the enemy once the A-10s had made a pass over an area. If that wasn't enough, the planes also carried rockets and bombs. Ben thought of them as crowd pleasers.

The pass wound through mountains that looked old as time itself. At the bottom of the pass, a creek meandered through, with the road—if it could be called that—crossing it on several occasions. The road dipped down, then climbed up as it passed through villages where the children came running to see what the Americans would give them.

"Chocolate! Chocolate! Pencil!" the children cried, putting their hands to their mouths in the universal gesture for *give me something to eat.*

The turret gunner on the team sergeant's truck reached down into an ammunition can bolted to the side and retrieved a small bag. Stephen watched him open it and throw small wrapped pieces of candy out to the children. He asked the team sergeant, "Why are they asking for pencils?"

The team sergeant smiled. "The only words of English they know are *chocolate, pencil,* and *fuck you.* Guess where they learned the last one from."

⇥ ⇤

"Hey, OGA man! You see that?" the gunner called out. Stephen looked out his window.

The road was just wide enough for a single Humvee. On the passenger side, the rock wall rose straight up; on his side, the road dropped away to the valley floor, about 400 feet. Stephen had been avoiding looking too much—being this close to the edge made him nervous. He did look out and saw what the gunner was referring to—on the valley floor were several rusted vehicles, including an old tank.

"Them stupid Russians tried to bring tanks through here back in the '80s," the gunner yelled at him over the noise of the vehicle. "Didn't work out too well for them, neither. You might notice a couple of newer vehicles down there too—this is prime ambush territory. About one in five supply runs makes it through here, so we end up having to resupply Lwara by helicopter. Taliban loves putting IEDs out here too."

Stephen couldn't understand the joy and excitement he heard in the man's voice. *Why would the prospect of violent death excite someone? These men are insane.*

⚊⚔ ⚔⚊

Dusk was approaching as the convoy finally came down the pass and the land between the mountains opened. The vehicles stopped so the captain could radio the firebase that they were en route. Ben heard the A-10s check off station because they weren't needed anymore.

Once sure they wouldn't be fired upon, the vehicles moved up a slight incline to a low hill where the Lwara firebase came into view.

I wish I had come up with the idea for Hesco barriers, Ben thought. The idea was simple enough: Rather than fill thousands of sandbags or erect concrete walls to provide protection for a base, put the barriers wherever you wanted them and fill them with dirt or sand to have an almost impermeable wall. A Hesco barrier is a collapsible basket with black or gray felt attached to it. They were delivered in pallets, and a row of six, once stretched out and filled, formed a wall roughly twenty-four feet long and six feet high.

Hescoes surrounded the tiny firebase, with a road leading to the main gate that was guarded once again by Afghans. The Afghans guarding this base were different from those protecting the larger base at Orgun-E, however—they had the rougher look of local tribes. These were referred to as Afghan Security Forces, and they were hired and trained by whichever unit was in the area.

The biggest problem the US Army found with training Afghans was that there wasn't a notion of nationality—tribal allegiances were ancient, and the only time the tribes worked together was to fight a foreign invader. Because of this, if a platoon from the northern part of Afghanistan was sent to an area that was primarily Pashtu, there were serious issues. To Ben it felt as if a platoon from New York was sent to his home state of Mississippi and everyone hated each other, but what did he know. Then again, he thought, if a bunch of New Yorkers showed up in his hometown and started bossing everyone around, there would be significant trouble.

⊨╪╪⊨

The vehicles were parked and everyone began refilling the trucks with fuel, food, water, and ammunition. Captain Rodriguez motioned to Ben and Stephen, and they followed him into a low building.

Inside was an almost carbon copy of the operations center at Orgun-E. Wooden tables, radios, laptops, maps on the walls. A few pictures of family and a couple of pictures of scantily clad women. A calendar was pinned to a plywood wall that showed the team had two months left to go judging by a date in August with several red rings around it.

"Rod, what's up my man?" another captain called out as they entered.

"Good to see you, brother," Captain Rodriguez said.

The two man-hugged, that unique show of affection that was a hug but not quite intimate, with hands clasped between them as they pounded each other on the back.

When they finished, the other captain said, "I'm John. Welcome to Lwara, boys." He had a quiet Southern tone to his voice. "You two must be the reason for all this fuss."

Ben stepped up, shook John's hand. "I'm Ben, sir. This is Stephen, and I believe you can blame him for most of it."

Stephen said, "That's right, gentlemen. I accept the blame. May we discuss what is happening tomorrow?"

John looked the two of them over, then turned back to Rodriguez. "While y'all were en route, we got another message from HQ. We got the same message you did, about giving these guys all resources necessary, blah blah blah, then today we got another one: *ALL OFFENSIVE OPERATIONS SUSPENDED FOR THE DURATION, LOCAL PATROLS ONLY.* Looks like there ain't enough to go around."

He looked at Stephen and Ben. "What this means is, anything goes wrong tomorrow, we're kind of in deep shit. Y'all know we don't have any air cover for this thing, right?"

Ben nodded. *Nothing unusual there.* He was still surprised that they had air cover coming out to the base.

"All right, long as you know what the situation is. Come over here for a second; we'll look at the map."

They all moved to a large map that covered most of the wall.

John pointed to a square on the map. "This is us. Tomorrow morning, we'll move across the *dasht-e*—that's this flat area here—to the border crossing here." He motioned to a small group of buildings just on the other side of the border in Pakistan. "Then, whatever is supposed to happen, happens. My orders are *not* to cross this border."

John turned to Ben and Stephen. "Y'all understand that, right? If you have to go over the border, even five feet inside, you're on your own. I have to assume that whoever put this pile of shit mission

together knows that. I have to have general level officer approval
to cross that line, and I've heard through back channels that that
ain't likely. You get in trouble over there, we can't help you. We
have to respect the Paki border, even if the bad guys don't."

A cold knot formed in Ben's stomach. "Wait a minute. No help
at all?"

John shook his head. "Look, Sergeant, I have little to no info for
you. This was arranged by someone not inside our organization,
and I have been told to shut up and color just like Captain Rod over
there. When the two-star general in Kabul personally calls—he did,
by the way—and says make this happen, well, I make it happen."

⟫⟨

Ben walked out after they completed their briefing. He felt un-
easy, still not knowing what all of this was about. He had used the
secure radio to send a message to his team out in the west, just
to see how they were doing. The reply *ALL GOOD, MOVING OUT
SOON* came back shortly. He wished he was with them, not doing...*whatever* this was.

A bald mountain dominated the skyline to the northeast. John
had mentioned that they just called it OP1, because they maintained a twenty-four-hour observation team on it. Ben had asked
was there any way he could go up there, and John told him find an
Afghan with a Hilux and he would drive him to the base of it, but
then Ben would need to walk the 300 meters to the top. "Oh, and
make sure you take a radio, let 'em know you're coming so they
don't shoot you."

⟫⟨

Once dropped off at the base of the mountain, Ben radioed the
top, letting them know who he was and that he was coming up.
Stephen had declined Ben's offer of accompanying him, deciding

to stay at the firebase. It didn't bother Ben at all—he had been around the man enough already.

After receiving the assurance that he would not be shot on the way up, Ben began his ascent. John hadn't been kidding when he mentioned to Ben that the climb wasn't for the faint of heart. Ben's nose was only six inches from the ground for most of the way due to the incline. He stopped to rest halfway up, and found himself face to face with a Claymore mine. He jumped back, then resumed his trek up.

Once he reached the top, he took a minute to catch his breath and looked around. Even as close as the firebase was, from this altitude it seemed almost tiny. A ragged bearded figure approached, grinning at Ben's obvious discomfort.

"Climb's a bitch, isn't it?" he asked Ben.

"Yessir, that sucked."

The figure laughed. "Been here six months now; the climb gets a little faster but it never gets easier. Name's Rick."

"Ben. You've been up here for six months?"

"Not in a row, man. We stay up here maybe two weeks at a time, rotate out so we don't go nuts."

Ben looked around. A sandbag bunker was on the side of the mountain opposite from the Pakistan border side. Several small craters were evident in the dirt, with some jagged cuts in the rock of the mountain itself.

Rick followed his gaze. "Yeah, we get hit a lot up here, but the sons of bitches can't aim for shit. These here," he said, indicating the craters, "was where they got lucky. Whenever we hear the incoming, we duck inside that bunker, or just put as much of the mountain between us and them as possible. Then we stick our heads up and see if we can see where the fire came from, try to call in artillery on it."

"Is that the border crossing up there?" Ben asked, pointing northeast.

"Yep. Just on the other side, that little village you can kind of see? That's the Lwara Bazaar. I've never been over there, but according to our Afghan friends here, it's like the Old West. Taliban, Al Qaeda, whoever wants to shoot them some Americans, they stop through there to buy their guns."

Ben could barely make the village through the shimmering heat and dust. "Great. That's where I'm headed tomorrow."

"No shit? Why are you going there?"

Ben grimaced. "Pretty much everyone I've met in the last two days has asked me the same damn question, and I honestly don't know. Somebody wants to meet me, I guess. I don't know who, or what it is about, but it's important enough to get all kinds of people riled up about it. I'm just along for the ride. Between you and me, I'm scared shitless."

"I hear you. You must be somebody important to get all this attention," Rick observed.

Ben laughed. "Me? I'm *nobody*, brother. Just another guy out here trying to get the job done. I've been in intelligence for a while, and this has to be the weirdest thing I've been involved in."

Rick studied him for a minute. "Well, brother, good luck. I'll be watching over you from up here."

Ben returned to the firebase and went into the wooden hut for visitors. A simple row of drab Army cots was arranged in two rows so twelve people could sleep inside. The air conditioner was struggling with the Afghan heat and doing a subpar job. At this point, Ben didn't care—he just wanted to get to sleep so the next day would come and he could get all this mess over with.

⟫⟪

Ben awoke the next morning feeling like he had a pound of dust in his mouth. *Fuck this place*, he thought. *If the Taliban want it, they can have it.*

He rolled out of the cot, walked outside, and went to find something to eat.

The Army calls all places to eat dining facilities. Great way to church it up, make it sound better. The dining facility was tiny, two picnic tables crammed inside a small concrete building with half the room devoted to the actual cooking. An Afghan was cleaning out a pot as he walked in. A television mounted on the wall was tuned to the Armed Forces Network, which was broadcasting a baseball game played three days before in Saint Louis.

The food was in large metal pans. Ben picked up a cardboard tray, selected two biscuits and then poured gravy over them. On his way to the tables he grabbed a carton of milk and a cup of coffee. Three other soldiers were sitting at the table, watching the game on the television.

One looked at Ben after he sat. "You ready for today, man? Seems like you're the star of the show."

"I guess." Ben just wanted to eat.

The soldier grunted, then turned back to the game.

⊷ ⊶

After breakfast, Ben collected his gear and went to the Humvees parked next to the gate. Stephen was already there, heatedly talking to someone on his satellite phone. Captain Rodriguez saw Ben and walked over.

"Okay, man, you're in the first truck with me. It'll take about an hour to get to the border crossing, and then it's all on you."

"Why does everyone keep saying that? What about Stephen?"

"Oh, nobody told you? Word came down late last night that he isn't allowed to cross the border. Just *you.*"

"What?! Just *me?*" *What the hell is going on?* Ben thought. The cold knot from the day before turned into a boulder.

CHAPTER TWELVE

"It's my goddamn source; tell me why the *fuck* I'm not going with him?" Stephen was irate. He had been certain that when the time came, he would be accompanying this little shit to the source's location.

For three years now, Stephen's status had been assured as a good field operative, even though he was getting long in the tooth. He had drifted for a while in the '90s, the Cold War over and the fun gone. Everything on the agenda was domestic; suddenly no one cared what was happening overseas. Fucking health care. Fucking rebounding economy. Fucking *domestic terrorism.*

Then, out of the blue, in August of 2001, he received a message that came through channels Stephen thought were long dormant. He tried to get someone, *anyone* interested in the possibility of an attack by Islamic fundamentalists. Nooo, everyone laughed that one off, bunch of camel jockeys can't operate a computer, live in caves—how the hell are they going to attack *us?*

After the day they did, Stephen's star began to rise again. He relied completely on the source, never telling a soul who he suspected it might be. There was no way it could be him. The intelligence had been reliable almost to a fault over the last three years, and Stephen thought there was only one man it could be. He had not had a single opportunity to get anywhere near his source until now, and the morons in charge of him had suddenly decided, no, you aren't going because the source said he would disappear if anyone but Staff Sergeant Ben Martin showed up. At least he knew the gender now.

The voice on the other end of the phone was adamant. Stephen would be summarily dismissed if he tried to go with Ben to the meet. This happens in the intelligence field more often than not—a lower ranking individual has good information, and a superior decides that the information is worth more than the individual who obtained it. Stephen, like many others, had control taken away from him by someone senior so they could further *their* career.

Stephen began to say something else when the call disconnected. That was that.

⟨⟩

The ride to the border was as boring as the trip the day before. The Humvees and Hilux trucks arrived and parked in a semi-circle 100 meters from the border crossing. On the Pakistan side, two border guards warily eyed the arriving vehicles. The heat wasn't debilitating yet at this time of day, so both guards stood outside of the low brick building. The Pakistan flag hung limp on a wooden pole next to the building.

Captain Rodriguez got out of the Humvee and walked around to Ben's side. "Here we go. Our orders are to wait until someone shows to pick you up."

Ben nodded. No telling what was going to happen. "What then?"

The captain shrugged. "We were told you wouldn't be gone that long, so we are to stand by here on our side of the border and wait for you."

Ben walked to where Stephen stood. He stood with his arms crossed, eyeing the border guards.

"Hey. This thing obviously has you pissed off. What's the deal?"

Stephen didn't bother looking at Ben when he replied, "I think I know who the source is and why he is only asking for you."

"Ah. So, we know it's a guy, huh?"

"Yes." Stephen turned to Ben and smiled. The smile had no pleasure in it. "I think today may be eye opening for you, my friend."

Ben just looked at him. "Guess we'll see."

Two Hilux trucks came out of the bazaar about a mile from the checkpoint. Both had armed men sitting in the beds of the trucks. They kicked up a storm of dust as they came rocketing toward the Americans. Both stopped just shy of the checkpoint building. Two men in the traditional dress of the area exited the first truck.

One of them was younger, maybe in his twenties. It was hard to tell in this part of the world, as harsh living aged people quickly. The other man was much older, with streaks of gray in his beard. Both men were unarmed, and approached the border.

The younger man called out, "We are here for Ben Martin." His English was good, indicating he may have worked with the Americans or British at one point. His age meant the Americans more than likely.

Ben set his shoulders, picked up his rifle, and began walking.

The older of the two immediately said something to the younger. The younger one said, "I am sorry. You are forbidden to bring your weapons."

This surprised Ben. "Are you serious? You want me to come with you *unarmed*?"

The older man asked the younger something in their language. The younger responded, and the elder shook his head vehemently. The younger man turned, and with a regretful look on his face, said, "I am sorry, but you are not allowed weapons. If you insist, I am told you will not be allowed to come with us."

Ben looked at Captain Rodriguez. The look of exasperation and anger on his face spoke volumes.

"Tajiman!" he yelled at the Afghan soldiers behind him. Tajiman is the Americanization of the Pashtu word *tarjuman*, which means interpreter.

A middle-aged Afghan soldier ran up to him. "Yes sir."

"Do any of the men here know these guys?" It was a common question in this part of Afghanistan. Because the Special Forces soldiers in the area used locally hired men for their security, often the locals knew people in both Afghanistan and Pakistan. This was especially true in this area, as the region was known as Waziristan, and covered a large area that encompassed both sides of the border.

The interpreter turned and shouted something to the other Afghans. One of the older men stepped forward, scrutinized the two men in the distance, and called out to the older one of the two on the other side in a questioning tone. The older man broke into a grin and shouted something back. The older soldier laughed, turned, and talked to the interpreter for a moment.

The interpreter then said to the captain, "Yes, Abdullah"—he gestured to the older soldier—"is related to the older man over there. He says that they guarantee the safety of your man. He also swears on his family that no harm will come to him."

Captain Rodriguez turned to Ben. "Up to you, my man. You heard them."

"Don't have a lot of choice, huh?" *This had better be worthwhile, going in there unarmed.* He called out to the younger man on the other side, "Can I at least wear my damn body armor?"

The two men conferred, and the older nodded his consent. The younger said, "You may wear your armor but again, no weapons."

Ben nodded, and handed his rifle to the captain. He unsnapped the holster on his leg and gave up his pistol.

"Every one of them's armed, Martin. I trust Abdullah. The guy's a fighter, and he's shown loyalty to us more than once. If he says it's cool, well…"

"I get you, sir, I just hate going anywhere in this part of the world with no guns. Feel almost naked."

"I hear you."

Accepting his fate, Ben walked to the two men. They led him to one of the trucks, got in, and they all drove away.

⟨⟩

Ben sat trying to remain calm in the rear of the truck as it bounced over the rocky terrain. The only thing keeping him from completely losing it was the thought that if someone had put all this effort into getting him here, there would be little reason to just kill him or allow him to die. Not extremely comforting, to be sure, but something to hold on to. Besides, the effort—delaying missions, pulling him from his team, all the travel—what could justify all of this? *I'm nobody*, he thought. *Just another soldier. No reason for an elaborate scheme just to kill me.*

As soon as the trucks were out of sight of the border, the interpreter turned to him, pulled a hood out of his bag, and handed it to Ben.

"I have been instructed to tell you to put this on. Do not worry, it is for your safety as well as ours."

This is getting better and better, Ben thought. *Again, doesn't seem like I have a choice in the matter.* He accepted the hood and pulled it over his head.

⟨⟩

The two trucks continued their journey. Ben could feel that they were now climbing, going up a steep road. The drivers ground through the gears as they moved up what felt to Ben like a twisting incline. Several times he felt hands steady him as the truck rocked from side to side.

He did his best to remain calm, even though he was being taken to someone in secrecy as he was hooded and unarmed. He suspected he wasn't being tracked by anything—no aircraft overhead, more than likely no satellites, nothing. If he *did* die out here, would anyone ever know? But again, why would this person go to all this trouble just to kill him? The Afghan militia soldier with the captain knew these men, or said he did—so if anything happened to Ben, would they come looking?

It felt like two hours had passed. The air was thinner; the vehicles were straining now, in low gear as they climbed. Finally, with a lurch that caused several hands to reach out to Ben to prevent him falling out of the truck, they stopped. Ben heard the others moving, talking as they exited the truck. Hands helped him up and out, and he was standing on the ground. He didn't attempt to remove his hood, figuring someone would tell him something soon.

He heard someone approach, and the voice of the interpreter say, "You may remove that now. We are here."

Ben pulled the hood off and blinked as the sun hit him in the eyes. They were on the side of a mountain. The road stopped here where the two trucks were parked. A path led away from them, around the side of the mountain and looked to climb up even farther.

"Is this the place?" Ben asked the interpreter.

"Not yet, but we are close. You are in no danger, but the climb from here is difficult, so you do not have to wear the hood anymore. I don't want to bring you all this way and then lose you over the side!" He laughed.

Ben mockingly laughed with him.

The interpreter led the way as they climbed, with the rest of the men following close behind. The all had their weapons slung, and talked as they walked, completely relaxed. This comforted Ben somewhat—all of them had serious expressions at the border and in the vehicles, their hands never straying far from their rifles. Now, they acted as if they were safe. Ben hoped that meant he was safe too.

The path continued to lead up the mountain. From his view, the mountains stretched away into the distance, and some were covered with snow even at this time of year. He knew there were some in this region that had snow year-round—this chain eventually became the Himalayas.

Ben was in decent shape, but he struggled with breathing this high up. This wasn't even the highest point around—other peaks towered over this one. The interpreter noticed him breathing hard and laughed.

"Do not worry, friend, we are almost there."

Good, Ben thought. *I'm ready for all this weirdness to be over.*

⊷⊹⊹⊷

The path wound around one last sheer face, then opened into a small clearing. On the other side of the clearing, a cave opened up, one that Ben knew would be almost impossible to spot from the air or the other mountains. *Makes sense—you don't want to be found, this is a good place to be*, he thought.

He stopped and bent over, catching his breath.

He rose and took in the view. This is a sight few ever got to see: mountains and deep valleys all around, all practically untouched by humans. Except this one, of course—but then, looking around, there was hardly anything to indicate a people presence except for the path he had just walked.

The other men walked toward the cave entrance. The interpreter followed them, leaving Ben alone in the clearing. Two others, much older than the ones who brought him here, walked out at the same time. They both stopped and talked to the men going in the cave, hugging one another, talking and laughing. The two men from the cave looked at Ben, talked quietly for a moment, then walked toward him.

Both were dressed similarly to the men who had escorted Ben here: long white shirts over white pants and scarves covering their faces. Their clothes were shabby, dirty and fraying around the edges. Neither of them were armed.

One man approached Ben. His eyes, showing through the scarf covering his face, looked familiar. The man studied Ben for a few seconds, then spoke.

"Hello, Ben Martin."

An American accent? What the hell is this?

"Uh…hello?"

The man pulled the scarf away from his face. As he pulled it away from the top of his head, the man's nose and mouth appeared. The face…how familiar was this face? The eyes, deep lines surrounding them, the mouth with permanent frown creases at the corners. Gray stubble caught the scarf as the man unwound it, and the face was revealed at last to be one that had perhaps seen too many suns in this barren part of the world. The man was, of course, familiar to Ben because his was the face that Ben saw daily in the mirror, only aged a couple of decades.

Ben stared at his father's face.

CHAPTER THIRTEEN

"What the hell?" Ben stammered. "*You're* the one who want-ed me here? I don't…" He couldn't finish a sentence. He trailed off.

"Shut up, boy," his father said, grinning. "You sound like an idiot."

Ben's mouth snapped shut. He stared at William Martin, trying to make all this fit in his head.

"Walk with me over here. We have a lot of talking to do, and not a hell of a lot of time to do it." Ben's father walked over to the edge of the path and gazed toward the higher peaks in the distance. Ben followed, still reeling from the fact that his father was standing in front of him.

"Look out over there, Ben. You see anything besides mountains?"

Ben looked. "That's pretty much it. In every direction. Mountains."

His father nodded. "Kind of hard to tell where we are, huh?"

"Yes…" Ben replied, wondering where this was going.

"That's why we're here, son. I don't want to be found. I didn't want you to know exactly where I was, which is why I told them to put a hood on you."

Ben scoffed. "What the hell was I going to say? I have no map, no GPS, no freaking idea where we are." His voice rose an octave. "'Hey Martin, where did you go to see the dude who ended up being your dad? Well, it was in the goddamn mountains. Really? Any distinguishing characteristics? Nope, just a bunch of *fucking rocks*!'"

William watched him, letting it play out. "You done?"

Ben couldn't believe his ears. "No, I'm not done, you son of a bitch! Where the actual *fuck* have you been for the last twenty years?"

"Here and there. Go on, boy, get it out. We have serious business to attend to, once you get over your little hissy fit."

Ben realized he was just wasting time. He knew he could continue being pissed off, but his father would never react to it. Other than to belittle him, that is.

"Fine. I'm good. What is this all about?"

William laughed again. "Oh, I know you ain't good, son. You're too much like me; you're going to be mad about this for a good while. But like I said, we have a lot of shit to talk about and time is short. You can be mad when we're done, all right? Just let me say my piece, and then you can rant and rave, throw a punch at me, whatever. Okay?"

Ben sighed, knowing there was no point in arguing. He nodded, waving his hand in the air.

"All right. First things first—reason why time's short." William looked at him. "I'm dying."

Ben glanced up, his brows knit together. "Dying?"

"Yeah. I was diagnosed three months ago with prostate cancer." He grinned. "By the way, get yourself checked, that shit is genetic."

Hot anger flared up in Ben's chest. "You got any other news? You're secretly the Prince of England, or maybe an alien, something like that?"

"No, son. Nothing like all of that. What I've been doing for the last twenty years—hell, the last forty years, almost—is doing my best to keep our country from going to hell."

"Well, that's a good reason. Anything else? We done?"

William scowled at him. "Let me explain some things, smart ass. Like why I didn't stick around." He looked down, scuffed at the dirt with his boot. He drew himself in, then began to talk, not really looking at Ben. "I loved your mother. Still do, as a matter of fact. But you should understand something—I couldn't stay with her. If I had, things would have gone bad quick."

He looked up. Ben saw something in his face now, a desire to be understood underneath the rough exterior.

"I went home once, back in '73. I was home from Vietnam, and met your mother at a skating rink outside of Black Creek. Place probably isn't even there anymore, but back then it was a place where young people went. The wild and crazy times the rest of the country was experiencing hadn't made its way down to Mississippi yet, and people still went to church socials and skating rinks to hang out. The church deacons who chaperoned these events probably suspected there was booze, maybe a little grass, but for the most part it was wholesome.

"I was having a hard time. My time in the Army was almost up, and I had been talking to some spooks in Saigon before I rotated back to the States. My father had been in the OSS back during World War II, and I was a legacy. I had skipped the draft and enlisted to get a good job in the Army, against my mom's wishes—she thought I should have gone on to college, but I knew going to school would have been a huge waste of time. She knew I had too much of my dad in me, and trying to get me to go to college was her attempt to get me to change. I see the bloodline continues, huh?"

Ben looked at him, not saying a word.

"Yep. Anyway, the spooks got their hooks in me good while I was in Saigon. I was home, thinking about career choices and having a hard time of it, like I said. My dad was gone by then, just my mother left. I was twenty-one years old, a veteran from an unpopular war, and employment opportunities in Mississippi were scarce.

"So, one night, I drank half a bottle of the good stuff and cruised down to the skating rink. I ran into some folks I knew who were going to Ole Miss. I could tell they were looking at me like I had horns growing out of my head, having heard their professors tell them how fucked up veterans were. Funny thing, that was one aspect of the times that made it to Mississippi back then.

"I said screw it and went inside. Maybe there were people I could actually talk to in there. As soon as I walked in, though, I swear to God I saw the most beautiful creature on earth—your mother."

He leaned back, remembering.

"Lord, she was gorgeous." He looked at Ben now, reveling in Ben's obvious discomfort. "Sorry, son, I guess there ain't a man alive who wants to hear his mother objectified like that. You have to understand. I had seen other women, been with other women, but your mother—there was something about her. As soon as I saw her, I knew I had to at least talk to her. I walked over, full of myself, and said, 'Hello, darling. What's your name?'

"She blushed, and it was the cutest thing you have ever seen. Her friends all giggled as we introduced ourselves. I really hammed mine up. I was a little drunk, of course, but I really wanted to put on a good show for her. I wanted her to like me.

"I don't know if she was just bored with all the other guys trying to talk to her, or tired of her friends hanging on her—I tell you, she put all of them to shame in the looks department, and I think they knew it—but she said to me, 'Okay, Mr. Martin, do you want to skate?' Smiling the whole time. I told her I didn't know how, would probably fall and break something. She said, 'That's okay, let's take a walk then.'

"We walked outside and talked for just about the entire night. Time flew by for us. She told me how she was getting ready to graduate high school, had just turned eighteen and was also wondering what she was going to do with her life. I told her about Vietnam. Well, some things about Vietnam. You know what I mean.

"She said she remembered me from high school; she was four grades behind me. I confessed I didn't remember her, that if I had I would have never left Black Creek. She told me her parents' names. Ends up her daddy owned the hardware store there in town."

Ben knew this. His mother's father, Andrew ("call me Drew") Tibbet's hardware store was still there. As a child, he had played in that store for hours, running around and bothering customers until Grandpa Drew told him he'd whoop him good if he didn't stop.

"When everyone in the rink was getting ready to leave, she told me she had to go. I asked her if I could call on her sometime. She said, 'Of course, why don't we meet next Saturday at the park?' I told her I would be there with bells on."

He paused. "What happened that Saturday was magic. We met around noon, I bought us some Cokes, and we just walked around the entire afternoon. I had wanted to kiss her before we left the skating rink but didn't want to be too forward. Even though this was the '70s, that was still improper in Mississippi.

"This time, she kissed me. Right there in the park. I was lost. I knew I wanted to be with her, and she with me. Hard to explain, right?"

Again, Ben just stared at him.

William nodded. "That night was the first time, and doing the math, I do believe that was the night you were conceived in the back seat of a '72 Plymouth."

Ben's face contorted into a grimace. "How completely and totally romantic. Thank you for that—the one detail Mom left out. A goddamn Plymouth."

"I know, son. Life ain't always pretty, huh? What did she tell you about me?"

"She always talked about her 'pretty spy boy' but that was about it. My grandparents, Mom's parents, hated your ass. Grandpa Drew would go on about that worthless no account such and such until Grandma Eileen told him to hush."

William nodded. "They had every right to be that way. Your mother and I ran off to Memphis that weekend and got married. We came back to your mother's house and announced that we were now a couple, and Drew flipped his lid, calling me every name in the book, how I besmirched his daughter—I have to admit, I had to go look that one up.

"We gathered her things as he yelled at us. Your mother was crying, her mother was crying, I was just quiet. I knew he had a right to be mad at me, but at that point I had seen enough bad shit to know that life was too damn short. I let him yell for a bit, then turned on him and said, 'Sir, you may not like me but I am now married to your daughter. She is an adult, and so am I. We are in love, and I swear I will take care of her.' He stopped yelling for a second, saw the look on my face, then turned and went outside. Your grandmother helped Patricia get her stuff together, and we left. We went to my mother's house, and I had every intention of settling down with your mom. She had a feeling she was pregnant, just something she said she knew.

"Everything was peachy for about two months. The week after we were married, I reported to Fort Polk over in Louisiana to out process the Army, get my final pay and everything. I filled out the paperwork to show I was now residing at the address I had when I enlisted. I thought I was done.

"When I got back to Black Creek, I applied and got a job working on a road crew. Pay wasn't too bad to just lean on a shovel all day. Your mother got bigger with you growing inside of her, and life just seemed too good to be true.

"Problem was, it *was* too good to be true. I loved your mother to death, and my mom helped take care of her while I was working. I had a lot of time to think while I was shoveling gravel and pouring asphalt. Vietnam was still on my mind, all the damn time. I looked around one day, and thought to myself, *Is this all there is? Is this all I'll ever be? Just another good old boy with a neck redder'n a tomato going home every night to his pregnant wife and drinking too much?*

"The nightmares were keeping me awake. I won't go into detail about them—that's a whole other story. I started drinking pretty heavy, not really going to sleep each night, just passing out. Your mother, God bless her, was the most understanding woman I have ever known. She let me. She let me drink and holler and yell whenever the memories got to be too much for even the liquor to handle. She knew I was in pain.

"Like I said, this went on about two months. Once day, I had stopped off to pick up another bottle at the package store after work. It was a Friday, and my plans were to finish this bottle and maybe find another before the night was done. I was beat to death, had stood in the Mississippi sun for eight hours that day, and just wanted to be left alone.

"I got home and noticed that it was quiet. Mom and Patricia were taking a nap, and I was relieved, to be honest. I didn't want my mom's look—you probably know the one—the look that says, 'I love you, but I could beat you within an inch of your life right now because you're being a dumbass.' I'm sure every mother on earth has a look like that for her children.

"I went in the kitchen to get a glass—I wasn't to the point where I was drinking straight out of the bottle yet—and noticed the mail on the kitchen table. There were a couple of flyers for Piggly Wiggly and the Ben Franklin store having sales, but what caught my eye was a plain brown envelope addressed to me. *SERGEANT WILLIAM MARTIN.* All caps, so it had to be official. I picked it up, grabbed a glass out of the cabinet, and walked out onto the porch.

"I poured myself a good one and opened the envelope. Inside was a single sheet of paper, words neatly typed. Words that changed my life."

He paused. "You want some chai? Some tea?"

Ben, having been engrossed in his father's tale, sat up from his perch on the rock he had been sitting against.

"I'm good."

His father nodded, and called out to the other man who had been squatting nearby. Ben recognized the words *sheen chai*, or something like that, meaning green tea. The Afghans drank it almost sickeningly sweet, so Ben didn't really care for it.

The other man returned from the cave carrying a steaming cup and gave it to William. William said *"Manana"* as he took the cup. The other man returned to a respectful distance away.

"Who is he?" Ben asked.

"That is Asad. We've known each other for twenty years, since I was here helping him fight the Soviets back in the '80s."

"You were here in the '80s?"

"Yeah. I'm getting to that." He sipped his tea, then resumed.

"So, the letter that changed my life was a simple request. Remember I said something earlier about talking to some spooks in Saigon? Well, at this point the war there was just about done. We won every battle but had lost the war. Didn't matter—there was something a lot of us used to say over there, don't mean nothing. War's over, don't mean nothing. Nobody back home gives a shit, don't mean nothing.

"This letter, this meant something. The request was to meet with one of the men I had talked to in Saigon, said he might have a position for me. The Agency—that's the Central Intelligence Agency—was restructuring from a Vietnam-oriented mission back to a wider umbrella to keep communism in check. The request stated that because I had done some work for them, might I be interested in continuing that work, not for the Army, but as a civilian?

"Of course, the letters C, I, or A appeared nowhere in the letter. No mention of anything like that, but it was implied for certain. I was interested—how could I not be? So, after I got the following Monday off, I went to Memphis to the address that was listed at the bottom of the letter, at the time it said to show up.

"There was no phone number in the letter, so I had no idea if there would be anyone there or not. The address was in south Memphis, around all the warehouses and factories. I found the address and parked in front of the building. It looked abandoned, but there was a sign on the door that said *DENNING IMPORTS AND EXPORTS*. The door was unlocked, so I went in.

"Inside was a woman at a desk. She asked if she could help me, and I showed her the letter. She hardly looked at it, and told me I was expected. She directed me to wait in the only chair in the office other than hers as she picked up the phone and told the person on the other end that their eleven o'clock was here."

He paused. "I won't go into any details here. Ain't nothing to affect the story anyway. What I will tell you is that they offered, I accepted. Only details you need to know are that they told me upfront that I would be gone a lot.

"I've told you my state of mind at the time, slowly turning into one of those fellas that just fade away over time. There ain't nothing wrong with it, I guess—lots of them in that part of the world, and we both know the world wouldn't turn without men like that, getting out every day and getting the job done. But it wasn't for me. I knew I wouldn't last there long, and I'd be doing your mother a disservice if I continued on that path.

"I went home that night and told her that I had been offered a government job and had accepted. She wanted details, but I wouldn't give them to her. My mother knew what the deal was— evidently, I had the same look on my face when I joined the Army a few years prior. I was off on a grand adventure, right? Only thing was, this time I was leaving a pregnant wife behind instead of just my parents.

"The first couple of years flew by. Well, for me, anyway. I got to come home to see you born, one of the happiest times of my life."

Ben snorted.

William smiled. "I figured you wouldn't believe that part, son, but it's true."

Ben said, "Do go on."

"Patricia was unhappy with me being gone all the time, and said so every chance she got. The few times I did get back to the house, she would complain that I was just doing it out of a sense of duty, and she could tell I was marking time until I could go back. She had me figured, all right—that's exactly what I was doing. Most men would have been thrilled to have a beautiful wife and son, a good life in the country. I wasn't wired that way.

"I was doing important things. The Middle East was an even bigger mess back then than it is now. At least now there are countries trying to help out—back then, the other nations were just pissed off because everyone in this part of the world was declaring independence and the big nations in Europe were losing all their colonies. Add the Russians trying to nose in everywhere, and you have one big shit pile.

"It got to the point that whenever I did make it home, all your mother did was beg me to stop and *come home*. To stay. Not just a few days and then off again. She swore she would do whatever it took to make me happy, and the last time I was there—you were eight or nine—I finally broke down and told her that I wasn't coming back.

"You have to understand this, if nothing else. I knew if I came home to stay, I would die. Die of boredom, lack of direction, something. I was doing something I enjoyed, and I just happened to be good at doing it. I didn't want her to suffer...well, suffer *me*. So, she filed divorce papers—this was the '80s, so it wasn't that big of a deal anymore—and I signed them. The day I left, I remember her standing there in the driveway, looking lost but determined. I also remember you not wanting to come out of the house."

Ben remembered that day. The stranger who said he was his dad was leaving and not coming back. Ben wanted nothing to do with him.

"That was that. Two weeks after that day, I was here. Been bouncing around this part of the world for a while now."

He shifted, stretching his legs.

"Enough history. I know you have a ton of questions, but time is getting even shorter now. I don't expect you to forgive me for what I've done."

"You…you think we could, I don't know, hug and make it all better?" Ben asked.

"What?" William exclaimed, his eyes narrowing.

"You know, have a father and son moment?"

"What the hell are you talking about?"

"Come on, old man, let's hug. Let's get the last twenty years all out."

"You're fucking with me, I see."

Ben snarled, "You're goddamn right I'm fucking with you. Nice story, *Dad*. Haven't seen your son in twenty years, you bring him up in the middle of nowhere and tell him a little bedtime story about how you abandoned his mother because you just couldn't handle domestic life." Ben was on his feet now, his finger in William's face. "How dare you, you bastard. How fucking *dare* you. Is this a game to you? Huh?"

William sat, taking it, offering no resistance. "Want to take a swing at me now?"

"Thinking about it."

"Stop being a pussy and do it, makes you feel better."

Ben's fist was curled, his arm drawn halfway back. He stopped. His arm dropped by his side.

"You ain't worth it. I could whale into you for the rest of the day and it wouldn't change shit."

He sat, angrily looking at William.

"That's right, boy. Can't change anything now. You want to beat on me for missing your first ball game, not being there to loan you the car, take you to the dentist? Go ahead. What's done is done, and I've already said I'm sorry."

"Actually, you haven't."

"I haven't? Then fine, I'm sorry. I still think I did a better job of being a father to you by leaving than by sticking around.

"Sure thing."

"Okay, Mr. Abandonment Issues, let's get down to brass tacks."

Ben was sure at this point that he was only staying to see what else today had in store.

CHAPTER FOURTEEN

"I know you have questions. I know we could sit on this mountain for the next month and you would *still* have questions. Believe it or not, that isn't why I brought you up here, to talk about old times. I just thought you deserved a few answers. A few is all you're going to get from me.

"I told you I'm dying. That is true. I went down to Islamabad a few weeks ago with some serious pain, and the doctor down there told me the cancer is inoperable. That's about the time I quit sending information."

He stopped for a second, and then continued. "It was Stephen who was getting everything, wasn't it?"

Ben nodded.

"I thought so. I taught him well. We...had a falling out a few years back. He's in it for himself, always has been, even though he has significant talent for this line of work. I fed him just enough to make his star rise, didn't I?"

Ben nodded again. Having calmed down a little, he asked, "Where have you been getting the information, anyway?"

William pointed to Asad, who was still squatting nearby, just out of hearing.

"Back in the '80s, the Soviets were pretty much killing everyone. They would fly over a village, and if they even suspected there were mujahidin there, they would destroy the village. Asad lived in one of the villages with his family, had no interest in fighting. Just wanted to farm, raise goats, that sort of thing. Be a good Muslim. His village wasn't too far from here."

Ben said, "Wasn't, huh?"

William said, "Right. Wasn't. As in not no more. Asad was out with his two sons and his herd of goats, taking them to the watering hole. Two Hinds—the big ass Russian helicopter gunships—flew low over his village. I was dug in in the hills next to it, observing Soviet movement in the valley at the time. I guess the Russians saw something they didn't like, turned around, and began blowing the village to hell. The two helicopters backed off a ways, and two jets came in and dropped napalm.

"I saw Asad running toward me, screaming his head off. He had no idea I was there. I made a decision. I tackled him before the Russians saw him, held him down, and got his two boys to come over as well. I hid them in my hide site until it was all over. Asad was raging and crying, as were his two boys. I was just learning Pashtu at the time, but I could understand words like *revenge* and *hate*. I knew he was in a world of hurt as he watched his village burn. The rest of his family, including his wife and two daughters who had stayed in the village, were gone.

"I talked to them as much as I could. I told them not to go back to the village yet, because the Russians would often attack a village, wait until the survivors or people from another village to come out to bury the dead, and attack again, to ensure they got everyone. Sure enough, two hours later the two Hinds came back and made another attack run.

"Asad tried to tell me he didn't care about what happened to him, but he had to protect his boys. We waited another day, until I was sure no Russians were returning. I helped him bury his family. Once we were done, Asad was adamant about finding the nearest Soviet troops and attacking them. I told him to wait, to think about his sons. He didn't know me from Adam—to him, I was a Westerner who had just happened to prevent him from getting revenge on the invaders. He didn't want to listen. I told him, what if I could guarantee his sons' safety, what if I could get them out of Afghanistan and somewhere safe?

"He finally calmed down and asked how this was possible. I told him that I was here to fight the Russians too, and if he would help me, I would take care of his boys.

"He wasn't in right away, of course. He didn't fully trust me until I got my guys to come pick me and them up, drive to Peshawar, and put the two boys on a plane to the United States. It was easier back then for us to get people out of this area, if it could be justified—I arranged it through a friend in the State Department who worked at the embassy, telling everyone that this was to guarantee a source's help in fighting communism. Magic words, back in those days—'fighting communism.' It helped that I was providing some of the best intelligence in the region, and I could get things done. Once Asad received proof that his boys were with distant relatives in Virginia, he promised to do anything I wanted. He's been with me ever since."

"Wow. So, you're good at taking care of families, huh?"

"Listen, if you take every cheap shot there is we *will* be up here for several months. Anyway, Asad is related to one of the biggest tribes in the area, and even though most of them hated each other, most of the tribes had called a truce to their internal squabbles to deal with the Russians. Asad began feeding me the best information on Soviet troop movements, logistics, and so on, plus he let me know when any of the mujahedin were going to attack so we could observe how they reacted. I was receiving crates of weapons, and Asad was helping me distribute them to the fighters. This went on for several years, until the Russians called it quits and left.

"Asad stayed with me, even as I bounced around the region. As my Pashtu got better, we could talk more and more. We actually developed a pretty close friendship, and now he's the closest thing to a brother I have."

He paused, drinking more tea, and resumed.

"When the Taliban took over in the '90s, Asad had no love for them either, considering them a bunch of thugs. When we came back here to Pakistan in the late '90s, Asad talked to many of the elders around here to get information about them. I passed on everything I got, but it wasn't until September of 2001 that anyone gave a shit. You know the rest.

"Listen to this part closely, now, because this is very important. You'll see why soon. I have some very important information, the kind that I didn't want to transmit. I told you earlier that I only gave some information to Stephen. I intentionally did not give him everything. See, while I've been here I've also been collecting information from other sources. The Internet is pretty damn awesome for that."

He gestured to the cave. "I had a satellite phone and modem connection in there before, with the antenna hidden in those rocks above the entrance. I got information from sources all over the world—not for use by the United States, but for use by me—all just in case Stephen ever decided to come looking for me."

"Stephen? Why would he come looking for you?"

"I told you earlier we had a falling out. Well, it was a little more serious than that. He promised to kill me if he ever saw me again. I responded appropriately, in the Mississippi way—I told him he didn't have a hair on his ass to do anything.

"That isn't all. I've been doing this for a while now, and information isn't the only thing I've collected. More on that in a minute. Give me one of your rifle magazines."

Ben looked down. On the front of his body armor, he still had his spare magazines in pouches arranged for easy access. He opened one of the pouches, retrieved a magazine, and handed it to William.

William pulled a similar magazine out of his pocket and handed it to Ben. "You'll notice this looks just like one of yours. It is, with one minor difference: The follower is a little thicker, because it has a USB drive in it."

Ben examined the magazine. It had rounds in it. "Does it function?"

William nodded. "Sure will, but you can only put twenty-six rounds in it, in case you ever need to use it. I would recommend sticking it back as an emergency use only magazine."

"Please explain why there is a USB drive hidden in a magazine for an M16 rifle."

"I needed something that anyone who searched you would glance right over. Nobody pays attention to magazines, especially if there are rounds in them. When you get ready to go back to the States after your tour is up, when customs looks at it they won't see anything. To get at the drive, take the magazine apart, pull the follower out, and plug it in. A couple of years back, a friend in Saudi made a few of them in different forms for agents to transport information they didn't want to transmit, so I acquired one."

Ben nodded, and then placed the magazine in the pouch where the other had been.

"What's on it?"

William smiled, a little viciously. "I told you I have been collecting information for a while. The info on that drive is for no one but you, to use when you are ready. You're not ready yet, so I had a tech guy in Islamabad rig up a little safety mechanism."

"Safety mechanism?"

"Here's the deal. Right now, you're neck deep in the Army. Have you thought about retiring?"

Ben thought for a moment. He had considered it, staying in for the long haul since everything with Lauren was going to hell. "I probably will. What does that have to do with anything?"

"You get two chances to access this information, in case you screw one of them up. The code to unlock this drive will be the number they assign you when you retire. It will be on the back of your retired ID card."

Ben asked incredulously, "You're giving me something I can't use for another nine years? Why give it to me now? Hell, what if I had said, 'Nope, not doing it, I'm getting the hell out'? And how do you know a code that won't exist for almost a decade?"

"Some things are best left to chance, son. I have been following your career, and I had my suspicions that you were going to stay in. I needed something that would ensure that you wouldn't leave here and use the information right away. The information on that drive will be devastating to Stephen...and other people, people who still have a lot of power. Too powerful for you to go after.

"About the code...for the last five years, there has been a code on every identification card issued by the Department of Defense. Each one is unique, but there is a string of numbers that indicates whether you are active duty, retired, reserves, that sort of thing. It's a backup in case the bar code on the back doesn't work. When you retire and get that code, you'll enter it when prompted by the program on the drive. The program is designed to access some, ah, databases that not a lot of people know about to determine that you are who you say you are. For example, if you just went back, grabbed a friend's retired ID card, and used the code I'm talking about, when the query came back with his name, the drive would lock up. You would then be shit out of luck. As you can see, there is a lot riding on this that I haven't told you about.

"There's also one other thing on there that I am not going to tell you about. You'll learn about it when you're ready. It's also an executable file, in its own folder. After you retire, go look up a Ukrainian in Memphis named Yuri Shevchenko; he'll help you out with it. If he isn't around anymore by then, just mention his name, and mine. Ain't many Ukrainians in Memphis, and they all know me."

He reached in his pocket, retrieved another object, and handed it to Ben.

"This is another drive that I want you to give to Stephen so you don't come back empty-handed. He's expecting something, so you'll give him this. There's good information on there, so he'll be happy and hopefully will leave you alone. You're going to tell him that you saw my grave, and one of the men here gave you this."

"Your grave? Really?"

"Yes. You need to convince him that I'm gone. The men here are going to build a burial mound out of the rocks so that when he directs an air platform over, they'll see it. Coordinates for this cave are in one of the messages in that drive. It's okay—we're abandoning this place anyway.

"I am dying, only have a couple months left anyway. Asad is going to make sure I am buried somewhere where they'll never find my body. This is what I want."

"Jesus, why not come in with me, go back to the States?"

"I considered it, but that ain't home anymore, son. I want to be buried here. If I came in, they'd just figure out a way to keep me alive longer. I have no desire to do that. I'm tired, and I believe my time here on earth is over. Now that I've seen you, I've done everything I feel I need to do before I go."

There was a slight shine to his eyes, and he looked away. "I have screwed up every relationship I have ever had. The only thing I have ever done right was my job. I can only apologize so much before it just sounds hollow. So. That's it. I'm done."

Ben didn't know how to feel about all of this. In less than forty-eight hours, he had been yanked away from a mission with his team, brought to the mountains of western Pakistan, saw his father for the first time in twenty years, and found out he was dying. Now he had in his possession information that he wouldn't be able to access until he retired. If he lived long enough to retire.

His father turned back to him. "Told you time is short. It will be dark in a couple of hours, and we need to get you back to your side of the border. Asad put the word out that anyone even thinking about harassing the Americans or anyone with them would meet a bad end. There aren't a lot of senior Taliban around here anymore, but there are some knuckleheads that may see an opportunity to get in good with them by taking a shot at you, so we need to hurry."

He stood and held out his hand. "Goodbye, son. I'm sorry everything happened this way, but we damn sure can't have everything we want in this life."

Ben stood as well, and took William's hand. "I've wanted to punch you in the mouth for the last two hours. I don't understand most of this just yet, but I think I'm starting to."

"Don't hold on to crap like this, son. I'm not worth it. Live your life as a good man, don't be like me. Promise me that."

Ben told him, "I'll do the best I can." He was sure he meant it. He turned and walked away, leaving his father standing there. Ben didn't look back.

⟻+ +⟼

Stephen waited anxiously for signs of the trucks returning. It was getting dark as a cloud of dust rose on the horizon. The two vehicles roared up to the border crossing and stopped. Ben got out of the truck, turned, and said goodbye to the interpreter who had been sitting next to him. The men in the trucks waved, then drove off back into Pakistan.

Stephen didn't hesitate. "So? Who is the source? It's your father, isn't it?"

Ben looked at him. He sighed, and then said, "Yes. It was him. He left instructions for me to give this to you." He handed Stephen the USB drive. "I think we're done here."

Stephen's eyes narrowed. "Done? And he left instructions? What do you mean?"

"He's dead. I saw his grave. The only reason they took me up there was to show me where he's buried because that's what he wanted. One of them up there in the mountains had that drive, and after they gave it to me, they told me about him."

Ben took a moment to measure Stephen's face. "I haven't seen him since I was a kid. Now, you're involved in me coming all the way out here just to see where he is buried and retrieve information for you. I don't know what this is all about, and to be honest I really don't care at this point. You said he requested me specifically. Not hard to imagine why, now that I know who he was. I was just a couple of days too late."

"A couple of days? He's only been dead a couple of days?"

"That's what they told me."

"What about the radio or whatever he used to send his messages?"

"I saw a smashed up set in the cave nearby. That must have been it. Which is why he wanted me to come get it, I suppose." Ben hocked and spit. "We're done. That's it. I don't know what else you wanted but you ain't getting it from me."

CHAPTER FIFTEEN

"That's it? You haven't looked at what's on this thing since you got it almost ten years ago? Not one single time?"

Ben finished the beer he was drinking. He looked down, surprised that there were five empty bottles there, with an equal number next to Reggie. As he told his story, Reggie had been handing him cold ones from a cooler next to his feet so Ben could continue. He had a pleasant buzz; he attributed it to plain exhaustion from the previous two days.

He belched long and hard. "Nope. Not once. Honestly, I was kind of scared to."

"Damn." Reggie looked at his own empty bottle, then at his watch. Two in the morning. "Okay, man, that was one hell of a story. You going to go find this Yuri Shevchenko guy, see what he knows?"

"Yeah, more than likely. I think he may have some light to shed on all this. Where's the guest bedroom? I'm about done in."

Reggie led them in the house and showed Ben the guest room. After bidding him good night, Reggie closed the door as he left. Ben was asleep before his head hit the pillow.

━◀┼ ┼▶━

Ben rolled over at 7:00 the next morning, sure his bladder was going to explode. After relieving himself in the small bathroom, he pulled on the clothes he had worn the previous day and walked into the kitchen. He felt like a nap was going to be in order later that day, but right now there was too much to do.

Linda had already left the house, and that wonderful saint of a woman had left a full pot of coffee on the counter. A note next to the pot read *There is no way I'm cleaning up all the bottles out back. They had better be gone when I get home. Love, L.* Ben smiled as he looked through the cabinets to find a cup.

A little coffee made Ben feel almost human again. He went back in the bedroom, picked up his phone, and walked out to the back with it in one hand, coffee in the other. He found Jamie's number and dialed.

Jamie picked up halfway through the first ring. "Hello? Ben?"

"Morning, sunshine, glad you're up. You weren't waiting on my call, were you?"

"Hell yes I was. This place sucks; there's nothing to do here. I've watched all the TV there is to watch and I didn't want any pay per view. I've already seen all the movies they got on there."

"All right, get checked out and start heading north. I'll text you the address where I want you to meet me. I think I might have a job for you lined up. Get up here quick, too—I have a lot of things to take care of today. I think I got you a job, too."

━◀┼ ┼▶━

Ben was leaning against the Blazer in the driveway of his mother's house when Jamie pulled up. He watched as Jamie got out of his car and walked over.

"This your house?" Jamie asked.

"It is now. I grew up here, and now that my Mom has passed on, it belongs to me."

"You mind if I stay with you until I find me a place?"

"Sure. Drop your stuff off inside and then we're taking a ride."

Ben parked the Blazer in the parking lot of KC's. This early in the morning, there were only two other vehicles in the lot. Reggie had told him that Karen usually stayed there until 9:00 or so cleaning up before she headed home to get some sleep.

The two of them walked up to the door. It was locked, with the *CLOSED* sign in the window. Ben knocked and waited.

Karen peered out and recognized Ben. She smiled as she unlocked the door for them to enter.

"Morning. I was just finishing up." She looked Jamie up and down. "This the fella you mentioned yesterday?"

"It is. Karen, this is Jamie. Jamie, Karen."

The two shook hands. "You ready to work, Mr. Jamie?"

"Yes ma'am."

"Good deal. You can start now if that's all right with you."

Karen put Jamie to work immediately, tasking him to bring in cases of drinks and foodstuffs. He happily set to his tasks as he had done no physical activity in the last few days and was, as he put it, a little stiff from doing nothing. Ben told him he was welcome to stay at his mother's old house until he found his own, as long as he pitched in to help around the place. Jamie agreed.

Ben and Karen took a seat at one of the booths.

"I think you'll be happy with him," Ben said. "He seems to be a good kid, ready to work."

"I believe I will," Karen responded. "I think he already noticed Jen when she came in earlier."

Jen was one of the servers, a pretty girl who was working to save money to go to Ole Miss the next fall. When she arrived, Jamie was obvious about not being able to keep his eyes off her.

Karen looked at Ben. "What's next? You plan to stick around for a while, live in your mother's house? I could use another hand around here if you want the work. Can't pay much but it'll give you something to do."

Ben shook his head. "I appreciate it, but there are a few things I need to do before I settle down."

"Like what?"

"Long story. I'll tell you sometime."

Karen raised an eyebrow. "Fair enough. Tell you what. Why don't you come over to my house Thursday evening and I'll cook supper for you, we can talk about it then. I would say Friday or Saturday but I have to be here on those nights. We get busy."

Ben smiled. "Little forward, don't you think? I just got here."

Karen laughed. "No, that isn't my intention at all. Just supper, that's it. I want to talk about your mom some, I feel like you might want to as well. This ain't a date."

"Sounds good to me."

⚔️

Supper was fried chicken, mashed potatoes, and biscuits—all the foods Ben grew up eating at his mother's table. He suspected his mother had filled Karen in on what he liked years before.

Ben leaned back on the couch and looked at the pictures on Karen's wall. One caught his eye. In it, Karen was being presented a medal by a colonel. Next to this picture, there was a framed certificate and the medal itself. He turned toward the kitchen and said, "What did you get the Bronze Star for?"

Karen continued what she was doing for a minute or so, and Ben figured he would find out soon enough.

Karen came out of the kitchen with two beers, gave him one, and sat on the couch near him—not quite intimate distance, but not unfriendly either.

"You know I was in the Reserves, right?" she said.

"Yep."

"Well, I wasn't anything glorious. I was a supply sergeant with the Combat Service Supply unit out of Memphis for about ten years. I had been in about five years when we invaded Iraq, and since Terry was back in prison I figured why not, and I volunteered for a rotation to replace one of the soldiers who had just had a baby."

She took a long drink. "My unit was running a regular supply route up toward Kirkuk. We left Tikrit around 0730 and were supposed to follow MSR Clemson—you know what an MSR is, right?"

Ben nodded. "Main supply route or something like that."

Karen took another drink. "Right. Anyway, this was in June of '04, so the convoys had started getting hit regularly, but not a lot had happened to us on the last couple. Couple of AK rounds, an RPG that flew way the hell over the trucks, that kind of thing. Regardless, I drilled the living hell out of my section, had them mounting the .50 cal, maintaining it, loading, all that with regularity. I had a twenty-year-old private, an idiot named Reilly who had joined the Reserves to get money for college and ended up in Iraq pissed at the world. I kept telling him that Ole Miss would still be there when the war was over. He didn't give one rat's ass about combat. He wanted to get the tour over, go home, and look for an easy piece of college ass on the square in Oxford."

Ben winced at this. Karen laughed a little. "Not used to hearing a woman talk like this, huh?"

"Not really. Weren't a lot of females around when I was out at firebases in Afghanistan."

Karen nodded, looked at the wall again. Her eyes had gotten shiny as she remembered.

"So. 0730. We got our convoy brief, then I checked my guys' gear and had them mount up. We had five trucks loaded down with food, water, and other firebase necessities. One truck had small arms ammo—that was the one truck that had any armor on it. The rest were just regular Army vehicles. We had a couple of Humvees with .50 cals in the turrets, and one Hemmett with a 240 bravo in the turret, so we had a little ass with us in case anything happened. The captain was in the lead vehicle and I loaded up in the rear Humvee. As a staff sergeant, I was the senior NCO. Reilly, my problem child, got on the .50 in my truck. Tim Lattrell drove; I was in the TC seat so I could monitor the radio. That was it for my truck.

"We left the wire heading straight down Clemson. We passed a couple of little villages, then the land started to flatten out to straight up nothing. It was boring as hell. I spent a good amount of time just thinking about what I was going to buy when I got home—I was saving money like crazy, and would actually have a decent check when I rotated back to the States."

She laughed. "You know what I wanted to buy, while I was day-dreaming instead of checking my sector like I was supposed to? A fucking Mustang convertible."

"Mustangs rock."

"Yes, they do, and I was going to buy the most expensive one they had." She looked at her bottle, and as she tilted her head, tears ran down her face. "I'm empty. You want another one?"

"Sure."

Karen got up, went to the kitchen, and came back with two more bottles. After twisting the top off one of them, she handed it to Ben and opened hers. She sat back down and curled her legs up under her.

"Are you sure you want to hear about this? You lived it, didn't you?"

Ben responded immediately. "Yes. Trust me, you want to talk about this. I didn't for a while, and when I found someone who could relate, it was like...I don't know, it was like I *needed* to. My wife—my *ex* wife—she could sympathize, but since she hadn't done anything like it, she didn't...she couldn't understand, you know?"

"Yeah, I get that. Honestly, I haven't talked to hardly anyone about this. Most men around here don't want to hear about a woman who has been in combat, done shit that *they* haven't done."

"Kind of limits your romantic opportunities, huh?"

She looked at him, head leaned to the side. "Are you humoring me to get in my pants?" She sounded playful, but Ben could hear the seriousness in her voice.

He held her gaze steadily. "No. I ain't trying to be the pretend sensitive, caring douchebag who's trying to get you in the sack. Right now, we're two veterans talking, that's it."

She sighed. "Fair enough. Where was I?"

"Route Clemson, daydreaming about Mustangs."

"Right. According to the PLGR—the GPS—and the map, we were about thirty kilometers from Kirkuk. We passed a small firebase, I don't even remember the name of it, can't even remember if there were US or Allied guys there. I remember topping a small rise and seeing a bridge way off in the distance. The bridge went over a river that was supposed to be roughly our halfway point.

"I do remember thinking it was weird that we hadn't seen any other vehicles in a while. I reached back and tapped Reilly on the leg to ask him if he was seeing anything behind us. He had the gun pointed to the rear to cover our six. You've been in convoys, right?"

Ben nodded. He remembered how much being the rear vehicle sucked, as every bit of dust and dirt kicked up by other vehicles ended up in yours.

"Reilly said something but I couldn't hear him. I think he forgot just how loud it is when you're in the vehicle instead of sitting up in the turret. I twisted around as much as I could with all that damn body armor on and yelled at him to speak up."

"'I don't see anyone, damn it!' he yelled back. I was about to chew his ass for being insubordinate when something caught my eye. A flash of light off a windshield about a kilometer in front of us. I turned back around, keyed the mike on the radio, and asked the captain what was ahead of us. He radioed back that it was just a couple of trucks on the side of the road. I asked him if there was anyone nearby, and he told me to stand by."

She closed her eyes and blew out a breath. "This is where it gets really bad real fast. This was the early part of the war, when they hadn't refined their techniques yet. As the convoy approached, an insurgent popped up from behind the trucks and started firing a machine gun at the lead Humvee. These trucks weren't armored at all. From what the after-action report said, the captain was killed immediately by three rounds that hit him in the face.

"I only knew that people were yelling over the radio. We were spaced out well, and when the first bad guy started shooting, all I could hear was that popcorn sound that automatic weapons sound like from a distance. I saw the lead Humvee veer off to the right of the road and heard its .50 open up, but at the distance and with all the dust I couldn't tell what was happening. The driver of the captain's truck grabbed the radio mike and was just yelling 'Contact! Contact! Captain's down!' Then there was a smacking sound over the radio and then nothing from that truck. Ends up the driver also caught a bullet and was wounded bad.

"The other trucks kept moving, but no one else was returning fire. I was screaming into the radio for everyone to find a target and shoot. These guys had never been in a fight before, though, you know? Ambushes were what the infantry and the Marines had to deal with. Don't get me wrong, everyone knew about that convoy that got shot up during the invasion and they had to go rescue that girl, but come on! That shit would never happen to *us*!"

Karen was crying freely now, not bothering to wipe tears away.

"I ordered Lattrell to drive forward on the left of the convoy so we could get up front to see what was happening. He was scared to death but God bless him, he did as he was told. I yelled at Reilly to turn the .50 around to the right side of the vehicle and prepare to engage when we got around the trucks. As we drove past, I could hear rounds hitting them but everyone seemed to be doing okay, I even heard some M16 fire and the 240 on the Hemett was starting to shoot.

"Problem was, nobody was paying attention to their training and checking 360 degrees. There was a ditch along the right side of the road, and an insurgent was hiding about fifty meters south of where the trucks were. He jumped up with an RPG and fired at the truck with ammo on it. I think he picked the first truck he saw, and it just happened to be the most explosive one. The grenade hit the side and must have set off the mortar rounds because one second the thing was moving steadily, then there was a flash and a ton of dust… When it cleared, the cab was the only thing recognizable. Private Sullivan, who had been firing the 240 bravo on top of the truck, was killed outright. Specialist Danielle Jones, poor little thing, fell out of the truck on fire. She…she was…shit. She was burning alive."

Karen put her hands on her face. She sobbed for a few seconds. Ben knew better than to say anything.

Karen wiped her tears away, mostly just to make room for new ones. She steadied herself, took a deep breath, and continued.

"The…the next part is why I got the medal. I saw Danielle die. I saw her, and for a second all I could think of was the pretty girl who joined the Reserves out of high school but was planning to go full active duty because she liked the Army. She wasn't a beauty queen, she didn't sleep around; she worked hard and everyone liked her.

The first sergeant treated her like her own daughter. Everyone loved that girl, and seeing her fall out of that truck while *fucking burning alive* just...I don't know...something snapped in me.

"We finally got to the front of the convoy. I didn't realize that the two bad guys had been joined by three more. I looked to my right and I saw the captain's vehicle in the ditch. I told Lattrell to swing the vehicle wide. He told me later that I was screaming like I was possessed. I hit Reilly in the leg and told him to open up on the enemy trucks that were now in front of us. One of the bastards saw us and swung his AK to start shooting in our direction. I had my M16 out the window of the Humvee and was firing when I felt something splash on my face.

"I wiped at it and my glove was bloody. All I could think of was, *Oh God, I'm hit.* I heard a thump in the back and what sounded like groaning. I looked at the rear of the vehicle and saw Reilly had fallen inside the vehicle with his hand grabbing his neck, blood pouring out. I yelled at Lattrell to put it in reverse to get us some room. While he drove, I got out of my seat as best I could with all that damn gear on, pulled out a bandage and pressed it to Reilly's neck, yelling at him to put pressure on it.

"Then I think I did the craziest thing I had ever done in my life. I pulled myself up into the turret, got behind the .50, and just started shooting those two trucks on the side of the road. Great thing about a fifty cal machine gun, you know? They shoot through everything."

Karen wasn't crying anymore. Ben looked at her, knowing how she felt. It was something that no man or woman who has never known combat could understand.

"I...just kind of blanked for a bit. I yelled at Lattrell to drive back toward the enemy vehicles. He had to swerve because the convoy trucks had advanced a little. When we got back in sight of the bad guys, I opened up. I was screaming my head off. I couldn't talk for a couple of days. I pressed that butterfly trigger down and held it. I moved the gun back and forth until none of the insurgents moved. I ran out of ammo and was loading a new belt when I realized that one, I couldn't hear anything, and two, no one was firing anymore that I was aware of due to number one. Two guys jumped off the third truck in the convoy and checked the bad guys to see if any of them were still alive. They weren't."

She stopped.

Ben was still and didn't say a word. He knew remembering this sort of thing was hard.

Karen wiped at her eyes again. "That was pretty much…that. I put everyone out in a perimeter around the vehicles and waited for help to arrive. We got some Apaches on station to cover us until the QRF from the nearest firebase arrived, and they got us back to their FOB. They gave everyone medical attention, and Reilly recovered.

"Two months later I got my Bronze Star, right before we rotated back to the States. Your mother is actually the one who framed everything for me and insisted I put it on the wall."

"That's sounds like her."

She looked at Ben, her eyes red from crying but with a shine in them now. "Your mama was a good woman. She helped me through a lot—she told me she couldn't help her boy but at least she could help me."

She laughed then. It was a good laugh—not tinged with anger or sadness, a genuine laugh at a pleasant memory.

"I tell you though, she was pretty old fashioned. She told me she didn't think that women should be out fighting like her son was, and she was *not* sorry. I kept in mind that she was from an older generation and that was just the way she was raised."

Ben knew what she meant. He remembered being raised by his mother and fussed at more than once about behaving himself when his friends were misbehaving. The reason? "I am not raising a heathen." Very firm—no ifs, ands, or buts about it—and it was the use of her favorite word to describe people she felt were less than civilized.

"Let me ask you something. Have you ever talked to anyone else about this?"

Karen shook her head. "Not really. When my time came, I just got out of the Reserves. I still see some of the guys around from time to time, and I've heard they still tell stories in the unit about the crazy bitch laying waste to bad guys back in OIF."

"Well, maybe you ought to, you know. I got some help back at Bragg after one of my tours got a little bad."

"Honestly, I'm working through a lot of things on my own. Running KC's has been helpful, keeps my mind occupied. Your mother helped me so much, I could never repay her, rest her soul."

Ben looked down at his bottle. He didn't know what to say. He was attracted to her, and as they had been talking, he had felt the attraction strengthen. The problem was, he had been out of the dating game so long he had no idea of what to do next.

Karen seemed to be reading his mind. She smiled at him, and said softly, "You know, I'm not seeing anyone right now." She left it at that.

Ben thought on this for a few seconds, then looked at her.

"That's good to know. I imagine you probably know how I feel, but…" He hesitated. "Tell you what. Let's do this the old-fashioned way. I would like to take you out on a real date sometime. How's that sound?"

She laughed. "Wow. So gentlemanly, in this day and age. I like the sound of it. Are you going to court me properly?"

"Yes ma'am, I intend to."

CHAPTER SIXTEEN

S tephen walked down the escalator leading to the baggage claim at the Memphis International Airport. The flight from Atlanta was short—barely enough time for the aircraft to reach cruising altitude before it started its descent into Memphis. Regardless, Stephen was in a foul mood—air travel always did that to him.

He stepped off the escalator and saw Colin. *Excellent.* He knew he could depend on this man to be exactly where he was supposed to be.

Colin saw Stephen approach and smiled. "Looking good as always, Stephen."

Stephen grunted. "Is the car outside? I need a shower in the worst possible way."

"Of course. Did you bring any bags this time?"

"No. Let's go."

⚊⚊

Colin drove onto the I-240 Loop that led toward downtown Memphis. Stephen rode in the passenger seat with his phone in his hand. He could read Stephen's mood, as Colin had worked for him for some time now. Stephen glared out the window.

"What's the problem, Stephen? What happened? Why the rush to get back to the States?"

Stephen didn't look at Colin, continued to stare out the window. "I'm waiting to hear from someone. I think he may have failed to do the job that I paid good money for, and it's really pissing me off." He sighed. "Remember when you could rely on someone if you paid them enough?"

Colin laughed. "Don't know if that has ever been the case. It usually depends on the amount of money, doesn't it?"

Stephen grimaced, deepening his already angry expression. "I suppose."

"Talk to me, Stephen. We've worked together for seven years now. You called me out of the blue, told me to get to Memphis as soon as I could to meet you. Here I am. You know I was running that thing in Toronto that isn't quite done yet, but you made it sound so important that I dropped it and got here."

Stephen looked at him. Stephen was old enough to be his father, and in many ways, he felt as if he were. They had met in Iraq in 2007. Stephen was still a government employee then, and tired of the bureaucratic nonsense he had been putting up with then for over twenty years. He met Colin, a young Marine counterintelligence officer who was also starting to realize that the bureaucracy would never go away. Over cigars in the smoke pit one night, Stephen convinced Colin that there was much more money to be made as a private contractor. Colin agreed with him and left the Marine Corps not long after to throw in with Stephen.

Stephen trusted him, which was saying something. He didn't give his trust easily—he doled it out in tiny chunks only after serious consideration. There was only one other man he had ever trusted completely, and that man had royally screwed him over. Funny thing: That man was the entire reason he was here in Memphis, even though he had died ten years ago.

"Okay, Colin, here's the situation. Three months ago, I was working in South America on that thing I told you about, the thing with the governments down there."

Colin smiled. It was always a *thing*, never revealed in its true form, even when it was just the two of them. Had to be that way—never know who's listening.

"Something weird was going on with our accounts. You know I've had those accounts for more than twenty years; I established them back in the '90s when I was working with William."

Colin nodded. When he first started working with Stephen, he was amazed at how much money the man appeared to have. "Why even continue doing the job if you have that much money?" he'd asked him. Stephen told him that the agency he worked for fronted a lot of capital for operating expenses. Money was much tighter in the '90s—the Cold War was over and that hillbilly from Arkansas wanted nothing to do with foreign policy (except anything that might get him laid), so the agency's budget was slashed. Great thing about that guy's administration, though—because of his indifference to what was happening outside the United States, the money that *did* flow wasn't tracked too well. William and Stephen agreed to take part of it and invest it, opening different bank accounts around the world to dip into whenever the operating funds they were allotted were insufficient. The pleasant result was that the money they invested *made money*. Soon, they weren't requesting all that much from headquarters, particularly after the worldwide economy exploded in the latter part of the decade.

The problem came when that sanctimonious son of a bitch William wanted to use the funds to support the mission. Stephen had been apoplectic—*seriously?* The *mission?* From what Stephen had seen in his trips around the world for Uncle Sam, most of these people didn't *deserve* to be helped. They could all rot, as far as he was concerned. The world wasn't worth saving.

There was, of course, a falling out—to put it mildly. They went their separate ways, but due to their agreement earlier, they both still had access to the accounts. Stephen had considered moving the money from the accounts so William wouldn't have access, but at the time, it would have caused too many red flags so he left them alone. He checked them regularly, and oddly enough, there was no activity associated with them—except regular deposits from the investments. William disappeared after their last meeting, and the next time Stephen heard about him was when he discovered that William had been the one feeding him information from Pakistan. Even though the two of them had a falling out, with Stephen even telling William he would kill him the next time he saw him, that simple bastard believed in the mission enough to continue to provide intelligence.

"South America was good. Bogota was good; you know I love that place. Things were going well, and one day I got a text alert that I had configured to let me know if there was activity on one of the accounts I used regularly while I was there.

"Boom. The account had been accessed and there was roughly $5,000 left. Five thousand out of close to *600 million*. The account had a minimum balance requirement to stay open, and $5,000 was it. Basically, on Tuesday there was a balance of $599.7 million, and Wednesday there was a balance of $5,000. The rest was gone."

Stephen paused, looked out the window again, watching the buildings going by. They were close to downtown now. "You got the rooms at the hotel with windows facing the river, right?"

Colin nodded again. "Of course. Arkansas is lovely this time of year."

Stephen laughed. Being from the Midwestern United States, Stephen wanted a view of water whenever possible, and even the Mississippi River would do. He had always liked Memphis—the culture fascinated him. That, and if one needed something done, there were plenty of people in Memphis who were willing.

Colin said, "We have a few minutes before we get there. Finish telling me the story."

"If it had been just that one account, I don't think it would have been that big of deal," Stephen continued. "I checked all of them. All of them had the minimum. Every. Damn. One. Someone had wiped me out. I was sitting on maybe $50,000, all told. Fifty thousand out of almost 600 million.

"At first I thought there was a mistake. I called every bank. For obvious reasons, there were none in the United States; all of them had been set up overseas in areas where there wasn't much oversight. All I could think was, had they collapsed? What the hell *happened*? Finally, after talking to several of them—all of them giving the same answer, 'It was a proper transfer; we are sorry'—one of the representatives told me that the money out of that particular account had been transferred to a Swiss account and gave me the number. I had, ah, helped that representative out with a problem a few years earlier. A *Swiss* account—can you believe it? How goddamned clichéd can you get?"

Stephen was working himself up. Colin said, "Come on now, calm down and tell me the rest."

Stephen closed his eyes and pinched the bridge of his nose. "The Swiss account was inaccessible. Completely. Security and secrecy has always been their thing. All I had was an account number. All I *have* is an account number."

He opened his eyes and sighed. "Well, I have an account number and a good idea of what happened."

Colin maneuvered the car across the A.W. Willis Bridge to Mud Island. Their hotel was named the Mississippi River Inn, a completely renovated hotel that had an Old South charm to it. Colin knew Stephen liked amenities wherever he stayed, and this hotel had plenty. They checked in and Stephen told Colin to meet him on the rooftop terrace once he settled in.

The rooftop had a spectacular view of the river and downtown Memphis. When Colin arrived two hours later, Stephen was already there with a drink and watching barges go by on the river. Colin ordered a drink for himself and joined Stephen at his table.

"This is the perfect time of year to be up here," Stephen said as Colin took a seat. "The mosquitoes won't be out in force for another couple of weeks and it's actually pleasant. It hasn't gotten hot enough yet for the river to stink to high heaven."

Colin didn't respond. Stephen was always like this—never straight to business, always making an observation or two. Colin knew better than to ask him to get on with it.

Stephen looked at him. "You're impatient, I see. You always have been. That's okay, I have more information for you."

He pulled out the phone he had been holding in the car. "I received a text about a half hour ago. My source is telling me that the man I'm interested in is more than likely headed to Mexico. Or somewhere out West...who knows. I find this information suspect."

"Okay. First thing I'd like to know—who is this man you are having followed?"

An evil grin split Stephen's face. "William Martin's son. His name is Benjamin. I have a suspicion that he is involved in the money but I have no proof, no idea, nothing. I'm having him followed to see what he does."

Colin leaned back in his chair. "So...what? Why is he going to Mexico? You think he has the money?"

Stephen thought for a moment. "I don't think he does just yet. Don't ask me why, I just don't. If he did, I believe he would act differently. My source told me he went about getting out of the Army in a regular way, whatever that means. The kid I hired was in the Army and got out as well, so I suppose he knows about that sort of thing.

"I believe it's possible that Benjamin doesn't know anything about the money."

"How so?"

"Just a hunch. The last time I saw him was ten years ago, on the border of Afghanistan and Pakistan. If he's going to Mexico, I should hear something soon. In the meantime, we have limited operating funds. We need to do something about that, in case we need to move quickly."

"What do you suggest?"

Stephen turned his gaze back to the river. "We need to talk to the Russians."

⊨+ +⊨

Although not the melting pot that cities like New York and Los Angeles are, Memphis has always had a considerable number of immigrants. Being the crossroads of the South, many businesses operate in the area, including Federal Express, which has its headquarters there.

When Memphis was booming in the nineteenth century, many of these immigrants came up the river from New Orleans on boats returning from that port city and decided to stay. Unfortunately, this included the criminal element.

Colin hated working with the Russians. It wasn't even a Cold War thing—hell, he had been born toward the end of that debacle—he just found the average Russian to not be...*civilized.* He admitted to himself that was probably due to the type of Russian he had encountered in his career. It would be the same if Russians dealt solely with white trash and criminals and based their opinions of America on their actions.

Still...Colin detested them, but per Stephen, to go forward they would need help and the Russians were it.

The drive to the east side of Memphis the next morning was quiet, Stephen again glaring out the window. Colin was concerned for his friend—rarely had he seen him so worried.

"Stephen, what is all of this? We had some things going—"

Without turning, Stephen cut him off. "Exactly. We had *some* things going. Not enough. I'm tired of this nickel and dime shit. I have plans, plans that are going to require a large amount of capital. I *had* that capital until it was taken away from me."

Now he turned to look at Colin as he drove. "I'm getting too old to continue running around the world, scrambling for jobs. It used to be fun, now it's not. I was planning on being done with the whole thing, the job, everything. I was planning on retiring and burning through that money like a sailor on payday, not worrying about the next thing. Now, thanks to that little son of a bitch, I have jack shit to show for it all."

He looked out the windshield. "Take this next exit; we're almost there. Now be quiet, I need to think."

Stung, Colin did as he was told.

CHAPTER SEVENTEEN

Colin pulled into the parking lot of a four-story office building. There was nothing to distinguish it from others along the street—this part of Memphis seemed fully devoted to buildings of the same type. A few signs advertised different businesses like heating and air conditioning, accounting services, financial investing and the like. The sign in front of this building was blank.

Stephen and Colin walked through the front doors into a blast of cold air. Even now in April, the weather was starting to turn muggy, but Colin thought the air conditioning was a bit excessive.

A young lady sat at the receptionist's desk at the end of the foyer. She looked up as the pair entered. They approached the desk, and when they were standing in front of it, she offered them a dazzling smile and asked, "May I help you gentlemen?"

Colin smiled in return, but it was Stephen who spoke first. "We are here to see Dmitri."

"May I ask your business with Mr. Ibragimov?" she said, still smiling.

"Personal business."

Her smile faltered for a second, then returned in full force. "Please wait a moment."

She pushed a button on the phone in front of her and picked up the handset. Someone on the other end answered immediately.

"Yes, a Mr. ...?" She looked inquiringly at Stephen.

"Jensen. Stephen Jensen."

"Mr. Stephen Jensen is here to see Mr. Ibragimov." She nodded as the voice on the other end spoke. "Thank you."

She replaced the handset in its cradle and gestured toward a polished metal door. "Gentlemen, please take the elevator to the fourth floor. Mr. Ibragimov will see you shortly."

The elevator door opened into another waiting area, this one larger than the one on the first floor. The room was dark green, with a fountain in the center and various pieces of artwork on the walls. It gave the feeling that whoever walked into the room was supposed to be impressed, but not overly so.

A young man in a simple dark gray suit and a short, almost military haircut was waiting for them just in front of the fountain. When Stephen and Colin stepped from the elevator, he smiled and said, "Welcome, gentlemen. Please follow me."

Colin thought to himself, *I thought we were coming to see Russians. These people are entirely too polite.*

The young man escorted them to a set of heavy oak doors, opened the one on the right, and stood by it. "Please go in. Mr. Ibragimov is waiting for you."

The two walked through the door.

A gigantic desk, highly polished, dominated the office. The building faced west, and through the windows that ran from the floor to the ceiling, downtown Memphis was visible through the haze. The office was also intended to impress: two plush chairs faced the desk, with additional chairs against the walls facing the windows.

A computer screen sat on the left side of the bureau, and the man sitting there was reading something on it as they walked in. When they stopped in front of the desk, the man looked up, smiled, and stood.

This is more like it, Colin thought. This *is a Russian.*

The man was a true bear of a human. He stood at least 6'4", and the trim dark blue suit he wore did little to conceal the 220-plus pounds of what appeared to Colin to be pure muscle. Gray, almost white hair was combed back over a tanned, deeply lined face. He strode briskly around the desk and enveloped Stephen with a hug that looked like he intended to crush him.

"Stephen! It has been so long! I am so glad to see you!"

Stephen did his best to return the hug but was clearly out-matched by the larger man. He settled for slapping Dmitri on the back.

"And I as well, Dmitri," he said as he disentangled himself.

Dmitri stepped back and turned to look at Colin. He extended a paw to him and asked, "You are Stephen's friend, yes?"

Colin shook the man's hand and introduced himself. When he released Dmitri's hand (or rather, Dmitri released his—the hand looked like it could crush Colin's head if the large man desired), he noticed a large amount of scar tissue on the back of it. Colin saw Dmitri noticed and watched as the big man quickly shoved his hand in his pocket. The smile slipped, but only for a second. Dmitri turned back to Stephen.

"What brings you here, old friend? Please, please take a seat, both of you. Sergei! Bring coffee for our guests."

To Colin, everything the man said was an exclamation.

The young man in the dark gray suit left the room and returned shortly with a pot and three cups. He poured steaming coffee into the three mugs as the men took their seats.

Back behind the desk, Dmitri accepted his coffee, blew on it, and sipped. He nodded at Sergei dismissively, and Sergei left the room, closing the door as he went. He waited for Stephen and Colin to put cream and sugar in their coffee. He now looked at them, eyebrows raised.

"Good, yes? I get the beans from a Jamaican importer down on Union. They are ground fresh daily."

Stephen nodded his agreement, tasted his coffee, made the appropriate sounds of enjoyment, and placed the cup on a side table next to the chair. He leaned back and fixed his gaze on Dmitri.

"As much as I would like for this to be a social call, Dmitri, it is not. I come asking for your help."

Dmitri nodded, leaning back in his own chair. "I thought as much, Stephen. You are too busy a man to be paying social visits."

Now that business was being conducted, Colin noticed that the jovial tone was gone from the Russian's voice.

"Simply put, I have a business proposition for you that has the potential to be extremely lucrative." Stephen leaned forward, holding Dmitri's eyes with his own.

Dmitri didn't drop his eyes, merely asked, "How lucrative?"

"Roughly sixty million, give or take."

Dmitri didn't respond. His eyes went to the ceiling now, contemplating the figure. He said, "Why so much? How is the risk? And most importantly, what do you require from me?"

Stephen smiled at him. "Dmitri, the risk is significant, but not necessarily unavoidable. I believe—no, I *know* this is worth the risk. Basically, what I want is what has been stolen from me, and in return for your assistance I will give you ten percent. I do believe that has been our arrangement for the last several years."

Dmitri laughed at this, the jovial tone sliding back into his voice. "Yes, my friend, it has. We have helped one another numerous times. Am I to assume you need financial assistance as well, since you are offering a percentage of something you don't currently have?"

"Yes. What I will require is money and people to help. The situation could get...dirty. I'm hoping to avoid that. I haven't done anything in the United States in a while, and I prefer this to be as low key as possible. I feel I can assume you are in agreement on this?"

"There are many assumptions in this conversation, Stephen, the primary one being that I am willing to help you."

If Stephen was shocked by this, he gave no sign. To Colin, Stephen seemed so certain that the Russians would help him that the thought that they might not had never occurred to him.

Dmitri sat, the smile still splitting that tanned face.

After a moment of silence, Stephen asked, "Well, are you going to? I'm not going to beg. You know me better than that." He stood. In Russian, he said, "As a matter of fact, if you aren't, we're done here." Stephen switched back to English. "Let's be on our way, Colin."

Dmitri's smile finally reached his eyes, and a look of amusement replaced the hard grin.

"Sit down, Stephen. I see you remember your Russian, very nice! And the use of polite words, too! You know I will assist you in any way I can. I have never been able to resist playing with you. You are so *serious* all the time!" He laughed. "Tell me what you need."

Noon traffic was heavy as they returned to the hotel. Stephen's mood seemed lighter than it had been earlier that morning. Colin could tell the wheels were now turning in Stephen's mind as he worked out his plan.

"I have to admit, that wasn't what I expected. The Russians I dealt with in Toronto weren't anything like those guys," he said as he drove.

Stephen snorted. "What, track suits and gold chains? Shitty prison tattoos and cheap cigarettes? Those guys are around, and they have their uses. Dmitri has moved on from the thug life and doesn't allow his inner circle to dress like that. Of course, he still knows where to find them when he needs them."

"What's his story, anyway? What's going on with his hand? That was a hell of a scar."

Stephen chuckled. "A few years back, Dmitri attempted to get any visible tattoos removed by laser. His entire torso was covered—his arms, neck, everything. Notice how that collar on his shirt was a little high? He did a lot of time in the gulag back in Soviet Russia, and had the tattoos to prove it. He had a large crown on the backs of both hands that indicated he was a leader in the criminal world. There was a knife running right to left that looked like it was puncturing his neck. That meant he was a killer who was available to perform hits. All those tattoos mean something.

"After he had been in Miami and then Memphis for a while, he decided he needed a new image and started getting rid of the tattoos. The doctors did the best they could—you would think that cheap prison tattoos where the primary ingredient was the guy's own piss would come out easily—but there is a lot of scarring left over."

"Wow. What caused the need for a new image?"

Stephen shrugged. "Dmitri wants to be taken seriously. He's an investor now, mostly real estate, some import and export. Over the years, I've tapped into his network for help, and he has gotten my assistance as well. We have had a very beneficial association, and that was the only reason we were able to visit with no warning."

⊶ ⊷

"Sergei!" Dmitri bellowed.

"*Da, pakhan?*" Sergei responded as he entered.

Dmitri grimaced. "Don't use that word. That is old shit. Mr. Ibragimov will be fine. And speak English—we are not in Russia, son."

Sergei bowed his head. "Of course, Mr. Ibragimov."

Dmitri studied him. He was new, one of the youth who wanted to be *mafiya*, a member of the family, like the old days. He was a distant cousin of his wife Anna, so he *was* family. He was earning his keep as Dmitri's assistant/bodyguard. How to teach this eager young man? Teach him that the modern Russian criminal does not go door to door, business to business, beating people for their money? *We don't steal cars anymore; we don't walk into a liquor store with a pistol and threaten the clerk. No, now everything must look legitimate, a patina of respectability that could disappear if inspected too closely, so the illusion must be maintained.* Besides, Dmitri had realized a while back that the real money was white-collar crime. To hell with the penny ante jobs—liquor store stop and robs, extortion of the local businesses, thievery.

Respectability. We must have respectability.

There is a fine line, however, between maintaining that respectability and not forgetting what enabled the desire for it in the first place. Sometimes hard men must do unpleasant tasks to garner the resources needed to keep the respect.

In this frame of mind, Dmitri made his decision. "You will assist Mr. Jensen. Take your two friends with you, those two you are always with. The three of you will ensure that Mr. Jensen is satisfied, as well as ensuring we are paid in full for that assistance. If there is anything that is ever unclear to you, you will contact me for guidance. Remember your loyalty and do the job well, do you understand?"

Sergei was elated, but contained his excitement. "Of course, Mr. Ibragimov. Who shall assist you in my absence?"

"Send for Anatoly. He will do," Dmitri said dismissively, and turned back to his computer.

Sergei bowed his head again, turned, and began to walk out.

Something occurred to Dmitri. "Sergei! Wait a moment."

Sergei was back immediately. "Yes sir?"

Dmitri frowned as he thought. "My son will probably want to go with you because he will think that doing this will make him respectable, that he can make his way in this organization. Sergei, look at me."

"Of course, boss. I am looking."

Dmitri's eyes were hard. "Do *not* let Joseph come with you. I do not want my son in this. Do you understand?"

"Yes, boss. Joseph is not to come with us."

⚔

Colin stared at the traffic as if it were an animal. *Pay attention, morons, your goddamned phones aren't that important.* He sighed.

"Things are looking up, huh?"

Stephen, as usual, was staring out the window. "Yes, they are. I'm a little hesitant to use Dmitri here in the States, but right now I need things done and done quickly so I'm willing to accept potential problems."

"Problems? What does that mean?"

"Put it this way: I'm going to tell you a story about Dmitri, not long after he first arrived here in the US. He was making a name for himself in Miami, mostly in strip clubs. The scam was doping up some champagne when high rollers came in—public figures like the mayor of Miami, city council types, government officials. When the rollers went back to get their personal shows from the strippers, they were smashed out of their minds and compromising photos were taken of them. Their personal credit cards were then charged outrageous amounts of money, something like $500 for a $50 bottle of booze, that sort of thing. If they raised a fuss or fought the charges, the photos were sent to their families, so no one complained. It wasn't a way to get rich or anything, but it fed into other means of making money.

"Dmitri was trying to become more socially accepted during this time, even though he was running several of these scams. He started to rise in the organization and soon had a few guys working for him. A friend he knew from the gulag in Russia told him that Memphis was wide open, and Dmitri sent one of his men to Memphis to start some business here.

"The man knew how to get things started, and soon was making money hand over fist. The problem was, Dmitri wasn't getting what he thought was his proper cut of the business, so he traveled here to Memphis to check on the guy.

"The man Dmitri sent was only sending about five percent of what he was making back to Dmitri, even though the original arrangement was twenty-five percent. Dmitri was understandably upset, and made two simultaneous decisions: one, take over business in Memphis himself and two, make an example out of his subordinate."

Stephen paused and smiled. "Listen, Colin, I have done some pretty bad things in my life, and to be honest, allowed some even worse things to occur. I must tell you that what Dmitri did to his man is one of the worst things I have ever heard of.

"Dmitri set it up to meet the man in one of the strip clubs on Winchester Avenue, near the airport. Dmitri arrived three days before he told the man he was getting there so he had time to arrange for the meeting. He hired a local contractor to soundproof one of the rooms in the back of the club and install some rudimentary audio equipment so the room would look like a recording area. Nothing complicated, just some recording equipment and eggshell material on the walls. Once it was done and the contractor had left, Dmitri brought in a hospital bed and some surgical equipment.

"On the day of the meeting, the man came in to the club smiling, happy to see Dmitri. Dmitri returned his smile, and the two began to talk about business. Dmitri gave the man the opportunity to admit he had been screwing Dmitri over, but the man brushed it off. Business is business.

"Dmitri offered him a drink that had enough tranquillizers to down a horse. May have even been ketamine, who knows. Not to say Dmitri didn't dose the man properly, though—he had an expert figure out exactly what it took to knock the man out without killing him. The man kept a ridiculous grin on his face as he began to slur his words and drool a little. He passed out and Dmitri's men moved him to the back room.

"This is the part that really gets bizarre. Dmitri had hired a surgeon to be on standby. The man was medically checked to ensure he was unconscious but still alive. The surgeon then amputated the man's left leg. The *entire leg.* The leg was then taken down the street to a butcher where all the flesh was removed and the femur was separated from the muscle and tissue and cleaned. The femur was then returned to Dmitri.

"Dmitri waited a full day until the man began to wake up. The entire time he waited, he sat by the man's bed in that soundproof room, holding the man's femur. He regained consciousness the next day, and the first person he saw was Dmitri, holding a long white object." Stephen grinned. "The guy, of course, asked what happened.

"'My friend, you had a reaction and passed out so we moved you in here for treatment.'

"The man, still groggy from the anesthetic, looked around the room, and then down at himself. 'Dmitri!' he shrieked. 'Where is my leg?'

"Dmitri smiled at him and held up the femur. 'Here it is, it hasn't gone missing.'"

Colin shuddered. "Jesus."

Stephen looked out the window as he continued the story. "I know. But that wasn't even the worst part. Dmitri then asked the man about stealing from him. The man was crying and screaming at this point, and Dmitri went to his side. 'Did you take my money?'

"The man, completely out of his mind with the knowledge that his leg was gone and Dmitri was responsible, spat in Dmitri's face and said, 'Yes, you son of a bitch, I took your money.'

"Dmitri killed the man by beating him to death with his own femur." He looked at Colin. "Don't ever forget: These men may look respectful, but to me they will always be animals."

━━┽ ┾━━

Sergei did not like Stephen. Being told to assist him was distasteful to say the least; however, Sergei knew better than to disrespect the boss.

He pulled his phone from his pocket as he walked to the parking lot and dialed. His call was answered within two rings.

"Sergei! What's happening?"

"Gregory. Get Philip and meet me downtown, at the usual place. We have work for the boss."

"What is this about? What are we going to be doing?"

Gregory was always eager. No interest in college, no interest in holding a job, but always eager to be seen as a tough guy.

"There's an associate of the boss who we are to help. Whatever he needs we will do. I do not know what this is yet but we'll find out soon."

Gregory lit a cigarette from a pack on the table. "What will we need?"

"Do you still talk to that redneck down in Sardis? The one who was just released from Parchman?"

"Who, Billy? Yes. Why?"

Sergei smiled. "We are going to need someone who can blend in with these country types, and Billy can. He probably knows a few others as well."

━━┽ ┾━━

"Hell, Billy, we can do that. Shit, that's *nothing*. How much we looking at making, anyway?"

Billy looked around the garage. Eight of his...*friends* wasn't the word, was it? Associates? *Compadres?* Acquaintances? That would do. Acquaintances. Eight hard, trash talking, whiskey drinking, dope smoking, tattooed convicts. Maybe twenty teeth between them all. Only thing they really understood was money and violence.

"Look here, assholes, the payoff is going to be pretty good. Don't know exactly how much just yet but it should be good. That Russian up in Memphis wants us to do some work."

"We covered with the law? I ain't feeling another stretch down at The Farm," one of them—Danny, Billy recalled—said, using one of the other names for Parchman.

"Kind of things they're wanting done, I don't think the law looks too kindly on," Billy said.

Danny considered this. "Well, if the money's good..." He trailed off.

"I've worked for these Russians before. They have their hands in a lot of pockets around here, especially with the casinos over near the river. I think the risk is worth it. Y'all better let me know real quick, though, if you ain't willing so I can find some other boys looking to make some scratch."

The men around the table talked among themselves as Billy fired up a joint. *I need something to bring me down a little,* he thought. *If the rest of my old crew wasn't still inside, I wouldn't even need to talk to these idiots.* Funds had been running low for the last month and then out of the blue—Sergei. God bless his foreign ass.

Danny stood up and walked over to Billy.

"I think me and the boys are good, brother," he said. "What are we looking at? Will we need any hardware?"

Billy smiled through a cloud of smoke. "Don't worry about a thing. I got everything we need."

CHAPTER EIGHTEEN

J amie was leaning against the outside of the restaurant the next morning, enjoying a cup of coffee and a cigarette. When Ben strolled up, Jamie grinned at him and butted the smoke out on his heel.

"Morning, Ben. Have a good evening last night?"

Ben stopped short. "Why you ask?"

Jamie laughed. "You were kind of late getting in, and when Karen came in this morning she looked pretty happy. Jen said she ain't seen her look that way in a good while."

Ben grinned back at him. "Well, nothing much happened. We had supper together, talked for a while, then I came on back."

"Hey, good for you, man, good for you. From what I'm hearing, though, if you break her heart, most of the town'll be ready to mess you up."

"Don't believe that's going to happen."

"You haven't heard anything else about that Stephen guy, have you?"

"No, I haven't, but I'm keeping my eyes open and I advise you to do the same." Ben looked at the door. "How's this place treating you?"

"Pretty good. The weekend is coming up so I'll see how that goes. I like the work, and that Jen is something else. I'm thinking about asking her out. What do you think?"

Ben considered. "I think that would be a good idea. Have you told her what you used to do?"

Jamie had a slight pained look. "I told her I was a veteran, but she doesn't know about the leg yet. I don't know how to bring it up."

"Shit, just bring it up, brother. There's nothing to be ashamed of."

"Easy for you to say. You got both of yours, you're a whole man."

Ben recoiled at this. "Jamie! Just because you're missing a leg don't make you less of a man. How could you say something like that??"

Jamie looked down. "Sorry man, it's just…you *can't* understand. I ain't whole. I don't know how to act around folks. Most people don't realize it because I have a fake leg and wear pants all the time. I act tough, like it don't bother me, but it does. What if she laughs at me? What if she makes fun of me? I haven't been with anyone since I lost it because I've been too scared to talk about it with anyone."

Ben saw the pain in Jamie's eyes. He was slowly getting to know this young man, and he liked what he saw. This was something he hadn't noticed before—that Jamie was hurting.

"Look, brother, if she laughs at you then she ain't worth having. Be honest with her. I bet you'll be surprised."

"I'll give it a shot. Sorry about blowing up on you, Ben. You've been really good to me and you don't deserve that."

⊨⊨

"Good morning Mr. Ben!" Jen called as Ben and Jamie walked in the back door. Ben was still trying to figure out when he became old enough to be referred to as *Mister* Ben. From the looks of Jen, Ben thought she probably figured anyone over the age of thirty was old as dirt.

Karen came out, wiping her hands on a towel. "Morning, Ben. You want some coffee?"

"Yes, ma'am, please."

Karen turned around and went behind the bar to get two cups. Ben looked over at Jamie. Jamie was looking at Jen with apprehension, appearing to gather his courage. Jamie met his look, and Ben nodded his head in Jen's direction. *Go on, man. You got this.*

Karen came back with two cups of coffee and Ben motioned to one of the booths.

"Let's talk a little and leave the young'uns alone."

Karen glanced at Jamie, nodded, and led the way to a booth on the far side of the restaurant.

⸺⟊ ⟊⸺

"You know he lost part of his leg in Afghanistan, right?" Ben said as they sat.

"Yes, he told me when he started working. Why do you ask?"

Ben shot a fast look over at the pair talking. Jen's face was an open book—it seemed obvious to Ben that she was interested in what Jamie had to say, and Jamie appeared to be struggling with how to say it.

"He's nervous because he thinks she won't like him because of it. Like he ain't whole—his words."

Karen took a sip of her coffee. "I don't think he has anything to worry about. After he started here, he's all she talks about. 'Karen, doesn't Jamie look good in that shirt?' 'Karen, did you know Jamie jumped out of airplanes?'"

They shared a smile. Ben loved her smile, the way her entire face changed when she did it. Lauren had smiled too, but to Ben her smile had never touched her eyes.

Karen looked at him. "Thank you for last night. I have tried to talk to others about my time in Iraq but this is the first time I've ever talked to someone who had an idea about what it was like over there."

Ben nodded. "It's good to get it off your chest. It'll eat you up if you let it."

"What did Jamie say to you outside? You looked a little upset when you came in."

Ben hesitated, then spoke after drawing a breath.

"I've known a lot of guys, soldiers, Marines, who have lost limbs over there. I can't relate, you know? I was shot at more times than I can remember, but never got hit. Hell, I have a piece of shrapnel in my stuff at the house that hit a sandbag two inches above my head once. After it cooled off, I dug it out and kept it as a reminder. Damn thing is half a foot long and three inches wide. If I had stuck my head up at the wrong time, it would have killed me.

"All that time, all that violence, and I never got hit. When I see some of these boys and girls come back missing an arm or leg, I just...I feel kind of guilty sometimes, you know? Like why them and not me? Same as my team that got killed up in Kabul when I was here in the States for Momma's funeral. Why not me? Why am I special? Was I a coward? Did I hide at the right time or was I always hiding?"

Karen reached across the table and took his hand. "I don't think you were a coward. That would make me one too, remember? I was never wounded."

A slight smile appeared on Ben's face. "No, you ain't no coward. Not after what you did."

⊷⊶

Jamie approached the table, beaming. He stopped short when he saw Karen holding Ben's hand.

"Hey, y'all, I'm not interrupting anything, am I?" he asked.

Karen drew her hand back and motioned him to take a seat. "No, we were just talking. What's up?"

Jamie slid in next to Karen so he could face Ben. He was obviously ecstatic, almost vibrating with happiness. "She said yes, man. We're going out tomorrow night!"

Ben laughed. "That's awesome, man! See, I told you!"

Jamie nodded. "I know, I know. And I'm sorry again about this morning, Ben. Sometimes when I get worried about something I kind of lash out a little. I hope you ain't mad at me."

Ben shook his head. "Of course not. I'm happy to see you're settling in here."

Ben's voice took on a serious tone. "I'm also glad both of y'all are here. We need to talk."

Karen and Jamie were silent, waiting for Ben to continue.

"I need to tell you about Stephen. Jamie, remember when I told you to trust me, that Stephen is a bad man?"

Jamie nodded.

"Well, now I'm going to tell you why. I didn't want to go into it while we were in that field because I believed time was short. Here's why you need to be careful now, because I'm about to get some information that could put us all at odds with him. Keep in mind that this is all hearsay. I've been told a lot of stories about him, but the folks I heard them from are reliable. People who knew him and my dad, the two of them worked together for a long time.

"Right before Desert Storm, the CIA was looking for ways to make our upcoming war against Iraq as successful as they could. A lot of people don't know that there are numerous different groups in Iraq, the primary division being religious—you've heard Sunni and Shiite, right?"

Jamie and Karen nodded.

"The Kurds are an ethnic group that Saddam Hussein's government had been trying to eradicate for a while. They lived in northern Iraq, and hated the Saddam regime. The US government sent several people into northern Iraq to talk to the Kurds and get them to revolt against Saddam, mostly to make the invasion easier for us.

"Stephen was one of them. He went in and convinced a number of Kurdish leaders that the US was going to assist them with weapons, air support, all that. The Kurds bought it, and Stephen's star was rising quick. He even met and fell in love with a Kurdish woman. She was widowed by Saddam's war against Iran in the '80s, and she may have even been in love with Stephen. I say that because who knows what goes through someone's mind when your country is in ruins and a foreigner comes in who can take you away from it.

"Regardless, Stephen was smitten. Doesn't sound like the hard ass I've been describing, huh? He was, though. Which makes the next part worse.

"Stephen was sent back to the States, and he began working on a plan to get her out of Iraq. You guys remember how short the ground combat was? Well, after the coalition stopped just short of the Euphrates, the Kurds in the north were attacking and were stopped by the Iraqi army. The support we promised never showed up. The Kurdish rebels were almost destroyed, and Stephen's woman—I never learned her name—was killed in a poison gas attack by the Republican Guard.

"From then on, Stephen had a hatred for the Iraqis and was starting to get pretty disillusioned with his own government. He quit the CIA but came back as a private contractor for them. I'm pretty sure he was working with my father at the time, but I'm not certain of that."

Karen frowned. "Why did he quit and then come back as a contractor?"

Ben laughed. "I know you ran into some of them when you were in Iraq. If something needs to be done that could come back and bite them in the ass, they use contractors. That way, if there's any blowback, they can just point and say 'See? Wasn't *us*, it was those damn contractors!'

"Something in Stephen snapped. Oh, I really don't think he was all that solid to begin with, from what I've heard. Losing his woman and seeing a promise he made broken by someone else probably pushed him over the line.

"He bounced around the Middle East for most of the '90s, doing the dirty work that no one else wanted. I heard he was in South America too, and even did some things about the terrorist groups down there. He really came into full-blown psycho after September 11. He was one of the first to run the black sites we had for Al Qaeda. I was told he was the one who came up with the idea to play the Barney song on an endless loop to get them to talk.

"The one story I heard that made me doubt the man's sanity was this: Back in Vietnam, there were stories of guys taking four Viet Cong up in a helicopter. To make them talk, they would push one out. If the next guy wouldn't talk, they would push him out too. Savage, right?

"Stephen decided to do the same thing in Afghanistan. He took three or four up in one of the helicopters the CIA had and push them out until the ones that were left began to talk. When he had what he wanted, he would push them out too. The messed up thing was he would then report the location where the bodies were and claim he had information that the Taliban were crushing locals to death so he could use it as propaganda."

"Holy shit," Jamie breathed. "This is the same guy who hired me to watch you in Fayetteville?"

"Yep. I heard even worse stories about him, but I think that one is bad enough. You see now why I warned you?"

Jamie nodded. "I'm glad you did. Do you think he'll ever come and try to find me?" Jamie's face took on a hard expression that made him look older than he was. "Actually, I kind of wish he would."

"Hold on, killer, he ain't the type you take on alone," Ben admonished. "If he comes this way, I believe all of us will need to work together."

CHAPTER NINETEEN

Ben parked the Blazer in the front of Nana's and walked in. He saw Reg sitting at his usual table and joined him.

"Damn, Sheriff, you ever do anything but sit here and drink coffee?"

Reg looked at Ben. "Sheriff's gotta take a break occasionally. What are you up to?"

"I've just been working around Mama's place a bit. What's shaking in the county?"

"Not a whole lot these days."

Ben nodded, then ordered his own cup of coffee when the server came by the table.

Reggie took a sip of his own, then asked, "How's things going with Karen? Heard y'all been seeing a lot of each other."

Ben grinned. "Going pretty well, actually. Taking it slow, all that."

"Good for you, man. So, what else you got on your mind? You done anything with that drive you showed me a couple of weeks ago?"

Ben shook his head. "No. I'm going to, I just wanted to get my feet under me here." He paused, then a serious look dropped over his features. "Listen, you know anything about some boys running around the county, pretty rough looking?"

"Why do you ask?"

"Well, there's been a few times when vehicles cruise by my house, slow down, then speed up when I come out on the porch. I know I'm still kind of paranoid..." Ben trailed off.

"I haven't heard anything, but I'll tell my deputies to keep an eye out."

"Thanks, man."

"What's he doing in there?" Danny asked.

"I would imagine he's getting something to eat," Billy responded. "Probably talking to that sheriff."

"You think he's talking about us?"

Billy snorted. "Maybe. I know a couple of you dumbasses haven't been real subtle when you've been watching him. How many times do I have to tell you that we were told to watch him and not tip him off?"

Danny's face screwed up in anger. "Damn it Billy, I ain't no private eye or nothin'. This ain't the kind of thing I do. You want him messed up? You want his ass beat? Then I'm your man. I ain't no good for this sneakin' around."

Billy looked at him and grinned. Not the usual good humor grin; this one showed what teeth were left. "We are being paid to watch. To. Watch. And then let somebody know what he does. There's good money in this for very little effort and I am *not* going to let you mess this up. You hear me?"

Danny turned back to look at Nana's and didn't say anything for a few minutes. It was obvious to Billy that wheels were turning in the man's head. Danny then burst out, "So when are we gonna *see* that money?"

"Shouldn't be too much longer. Shut up. He's coming out."

———

Ben pretended not to notice the two men who were pointedly not looking at him when he strode out of Nana's.

Guess it ain't paranoia if they are really out to get you, he thought as he opened the door and got in the truck. *I guess I should consider myself lucky—one of these days Stephen might hire some actual professionals to come after me.*

He opened the center console to check his pistol. Still there. Good. He started the truck, backed out, and drove down the street. He glanced at his rearview mirror and saw the battered old Ford pull out behind him.

———

"We going to follow him all the way to his house?" Danny asked.

"No. As soon as he turns off on his road we're going straight so he don't think we're tailing him."

This seemed to satisfy Danny—for a couple of seconds, anyway—then he appeared to think and then asked, "When are we actually going to do something to this guy?"

"When the time is right. And by that, I mean *when we are told to, so now shut the fuck up.*"

———

Colin noticed that Stephen's mood was not improving. He knew better than to bring it up.

Stephen sat with a glass of bourbon in front of him, untouched. He looked uncomfortable, as if he were not wearing his own skin.

Colin knew this look—he had seen it many times before, when an operation was not going exactly how Stephen wanted it.

Stephen cleared his throat and glanced at Colin. "Don't hover, son. It annoys me. What is on your mind?"

"We've only heard routine things from Billy and his boys. Ben is doing nothing that suggests he has discovered that he's sitting on a pile of money. All he's done for the last two weeks is work on that house and date the woman who owns the bar."

"And?" Stephen looked at the bourbon but did not touch it.

"I know we have had missions like this before, where all we must do is wait. Those missions, though, had many more moving parts...and the accommodations were a little more...amenable."

The Memphis hotel had quickly exceeded Stephen's budget, so the two of them relocated to one of Dmitri's houses in the southern part of the city. While not a crime-ridden neighborhood, it still reminded Colin of working out of seedier parts of Eastern Europe. As if to reinforce the point, a cockroach skittered across the kitchen floor. Stephen watched it with little interest.

"Sounds like you grew accustomed to more palatial establishments during your short time with the Agency," Stephen said. "You need to have spent more time in shitholes, son. Get the silver spoon out of your mouth."

Colin let this go. "And what of this Billy? Are we so tight that we can't hire professionals to take care of this situation?"

Stephen laughed. "Tight? You have no idea how little money we have. It was nice when the Agency was footing the bill, but now, we must make do. We use those morons because they're cheap and willing to do the dirty work that will be needed soon."

Stephen finally took a drink. "Don't you think I checked to see if there were any professionals available to do this? As recently as five years ago, we could have gotten this done reasonably. All kinds of talent with nothing to do. Then the peace-loving administration of the people decided they were going to start wars on two continents while proclaiming to the population that the wars were over! Now there's shooting going on every day, it just isn't in the papers or on TV. All the professionals are now engaged, and even the ones who aren't wouldn't touch something domestic for less than ten grand a day."

"I see that, but these...these *rednecks*...how reliable can they be?"

"Colin, you mean to tell me that you never used local talent in any of your operations? What's the difference now?"

Colin considered this. Yes, he had used locals to gain access to sources, had used and thrown away more than he could remember. But that was not the United States. Well, and he had the backing of the US government on those too.

"I just think we should be careful with these people," he finished lamely.

"We will. I'm making our dollars stretch a little. All I'm looking for right now is information anyway. As soon as Benjamin does something to indicate he's going to the money, then we'll move and take care of things ourselves."

Colin snorted. "I still think we would be better off by driving down there, sticking a gun in his face and making him give us the money. The old-fashioned way, as it were."

Stephen looked at Colin for a moment, then laughed. "We have to do this the right way, Colin. We're not in Bogota; we're not in Baghdad. We need intelligence, *solid* intelligence. We need to know the proper time and place to stick the gun in his face."

CHAPTER TWENTY

Yuri Shevchenko was not a hard man to find. A quick Internet search found several Yuris, but only one with the same last name. There aren't too many Ukrainians living in Memphis, and Yuri had a home in a quiet middle class neighborhood in the eastern part of the city.

Ben had found his phone number listed online (*that* was lucky; not too many people did that anymore) and called him. The old Ukrainian was hesitant at first, but once Ben explained who he was, Yuri insisted on a visit.

As Ben pulled into Yuri's driveway, an older man stood on the porch smoking. Ben put the Blazer in park and got out.

"Benjamin! So, I finally meet the son! Come in! Come in!" the man said.

Ben walked up the short driveway to the front of the house. The man was smiling, gesturing him to come closer. Once Ben was on the porch, the man embraced him in a bone-crushing hug.

"It is so good to meet you! You look just like your father!" Yuri stepped back and swept his hand toward the door. "Please! Come in!"

Ben wondered if the man ever spoke in anything but a shout.

"So…your father told you to find me. Why now, after all this time?" Yuri asked as they sat in the living room.

"I didn't come right away because I was still in the Army," Ben said. "Had a lot going on."

Yuri nodded. "I understand. Life! It gets in the way, does it not? But now you are here. Tell me how I can help my friend's son."

Ben pulled the USB drive from his pocket and held it out to the older man. "Can you help me with this?"

Yuri took the drive and turned it over in his hands. Frowning, he looked over at the table next to his chair and retrieved his glasses. After putting them on, he examined the object more closely.

"How am I to help you with this? I don't know what it is."

The boisterous volume was gone now. Ben felt his heart sink a bit.

Yuri smiled. "Wait."

He turned and looked over his shoulder. "Jacob! Come here!"

Ben heard a door opening and a slight, younger version of Yuri came into the room. He looked up once at Ben and then resumed his prior gaze at the floor.

"Jacob, this is Benjamin, the son of William Martin. Say hello, son."

A mumbled *Hellopleasedtomeetyou.*

Yuri took no notice of this. Ben saw the love for his son in Yuri's eyes, figured that Yuri saw no fault in his son's behavior.

"Jacob, this man's father was the one who brought us here to America. We owe his family everything we have. Ben needs our assistance and we will give it to him."

Ben couldn't tell if the words had any effect on Jacob as the expression on his face did not change, nor did the direction of his eyes. There had to be something interesting on the floor but Ben couldn't tell what it was.

Yuri passed the drive to Jacob. "Take this to your computer and tell Ben what is on it, please."

Jacob showed interest for the first time since walking into the room. He turned the object over in his hands much as his father had. He rotated the USB portion out of the green plastic, then looked directly at Ben. "What is this, anyway? I know what the drive is, but what is it in?"

"Do you play video games?" Ben had a feeling he already knew the answer to this one.

Jacob smiled, a little tentatively, as if his face was not used to the muscles being used this way.

"Yes."

"First person shooters? You ever use an M-16, M-4, something like that?"

Jacob nodded.

"In the games, when you have to reload you have to put a new magazine in the weapon. That thing there is called the follower; it sits on top of a spring that pushes the bullets up into the gun."

Jacob laughed. The laugh was deeper than his slightly frail frame looked as if it could support. Must have gotten that from his father.

"Clever. I like it. Okay, is there anything I need to know before I look at it?"

Jacob was opening up now that Ben had something that interested him.

"Oddly enough I have never looked at the damn thing. My father gave it to me and told me that I need a code and an Internet connection to get started."

Jacob nodded. "Okay. I will look at it offline first to ensure it isn't contaminated with anything." He turned and left the room.

Yuri was smiling sadly. "I know what you are thinking. He is… odd. His mother was pregnant with him when we left the Ukraine and came to the United States. She died when he was five years old. I have tried to raise him to be more social but he only lives on his computer."

"It's okay, Yuri, you don't owe an explanation."

"I've tried to shelter him. He has never quite fit in." He sighed. "I especially did not want him to be like me. I'm sure you know what I mean by that. Your father talked about you a lot, how you were following in his footsteps, in a way. How proud of you he was."

When he spoke next, his eyes were narrowed.

"Benjamin. You have no children, do you?"

Ben shook his head.

"Then you have no idea of what I am saying to you. *All* fathers want something better for their children—the ones who are worthy of being fathers, that is. It is a universal constant. My father was a Party bureaucrat and expected me to do the same. I had no desire to live as a functionary and joined the Soviet Army. I eventually moved to the KGB, which is how I met your father."

"You were in the KGB?" Ben asked, incredulous.

"Yes. Oh, don't look at me like that. I was no monster, just as not every agent in your CIA is a monster. I performed my duties until I could no longer consciously do them."

"How did you meet?"

Yuri sighed again. "That…is a story for another time. That story is difficult to tell, and I do not feel like telling it. Suffice to say I did not leave the Soviet Union on good terms, and your father William was the main reason. Someday there will be people coming for me. The Russians never forget, even now. Which is why"—he smiled evilly as he reached under his chair—"I will be ready for them when they come."

Yuri pulled out a dark green bag. The objects inside the bag pressed against the outside in a roughly oval shape. There was Cyrillic writing on the outside of the bag, with some diagrams Ben couldn't make out.

"You were in your army, so you are familiar with the Claymore Mine, yes?"

Ben nodded. Very familiar.

"These are the Russian equivalent, slightly more powerful. It is called the Chekov Antipersonnel Mine, and each bag contains two of them, plus the arming and firing devices. Your military has found them all over Iraq and Afghanistan. Somewhat effective against lightly armored vehicles, devastating to people in the open."

"Jesus. Why do you have them in your living room?"

"One never knows when he might need to dispose of pests."

Ben nervously watched Yuri place the bag back under his chair. "I'm guessing they aren't armed right now?" he asked.

"No. I have the safeties enabled in both. I have run the wires for both to the arm of the chair I am sitting in, and if I need them in a hurry, I take the firing device and go into the kitchen to detonate them. The kitchen wall is a solid concrete block, as well as the walls of the living room. Contains the blast, if needed."

"Effective, I guess, if the, ah, pests are in the living room, huh?"

Yuri laughed. "Very. A last resort, as you say. I have other defense mechanisms throughout the house. Growing up in the USSR made me paranoid." The grin that formed next was a little unpleasant for Ben, and in that moment, he could clearly see Yuri as a KGB operative. "Due to my former career, it actually was not too difficult to obtain the materials needed for home defense."

Huh, Ben thought. *And here I was thinking I had it covered with a pump shotgun.*

Jacob called out, "Please come in. I think the drive is safe."

Ben and Yuri entered Jacob's room. Ben had originally thought Jacob was in his twenties, but now he realized Yuri's son was probably in his mid-thirties based on his room—no posters on the walls, only a few pictures of landscapes or cities. There was a bookcase, filled with games and DVDs.

Jacob was hunched over a keyboard and looked up as they entered.

"The code used here is a little old, but there is no way around it that I can see. Whoever set this up knew what they were doing. To get anywhere, you must put your password in." Jacob pushed back from the keyboard so Ben could get to it.

Ben retrieved his wallet and plucked his retired ID card from it. On the back was the string of digits that had been assigned to him after he retired.

On the screen, Ben saw a simple prompt: *ENTER PASSWORD.* He typed in the numbers and hit *ENTER.*

There was a pause, with the familiar blue circle as the machine considered his input. The pop-up disappeared and a new screen appeared with two folders and a video icon. The name of the video was *WATCH ME FIRST.* After glancing at Jacob, who nodded, Ben double clicked it.

"Hello son." After all these years, it was a shock to Ben to hear his dad's voice. In the video, his father was dressed much as he was the last time he saw him, and looked to be in the same cave that Ben had visited over ten years ago.

"So, you finally retired. Good. You will see soon why I wanted you to wait. First, though, I want to tell you about one of the folders on this drive and what I want you to do with it.

"I plan on telling some of this to you in person when I see you. I've already sent out hints across the grapevine about my location and that I want to meet with you in the next couple of weeks. I'll tell you more about why time is a little short when we are face to face.

"I advise you not to be socially backward when looking at the folder marked *#1.* Try to use your brain, the one God gave you, and not like a lot of other people who are socially backward. I only bring this up because I think it will help you in the long run." A grin. "Again, as you may have learned, there are things that people try to tell you that may not be obvious until you think about them for a few. Once you've figured out what I'm telling you, I highly advise you to change certain things. You know, just in case somebody else gets their hands on this."

The three men looked at one another. What the hell was he talking about? They turned back to the video.

"That's all I'm going to say about folder number one. The other folder has some good tidbits about what Stephen has been up to over the years. Use it, or don't, I leave that to you. You may find it useful at some point.

"Be careful with him. I watched him turn from a decent officer into a..." William paused, considering. "Not a monster, but close. He's small minded and petty, but I think we all have the capacity for that from time to time. He acts in the interests of the country, when they happen to coincide with his own. The last few years his own concerns seem to have outpaced the country's and that worries me. He is very smart, though, so take precautions around him.

"That's it. I will tell you everything else when I see you. If I don't see you for some reason, well, I'll just destroy this thing and see what else happens."

The video ended.

"What did I just watch? Was he this incoherent when you knew him?" Ben asked Yuri.

Yuri shrugged. "He had his own way of thinking and talking, but this just sounds like rambling to me. Jacob?"

Jacob shook his head. "Maybe we should just look at the first folder."

He clicked on the folder marked *#1*. A single icon this time. Jacob hovered the cursor over it to determine the file type.

"An executable. A program. Should I run it?"

Ben nodded. "Why not?"

Again, the blue circle ran, this time for a few more seconds. A web browser page opened. Ben read the title.

"Well, shit. Foreign bank web page? That's interesting."

Jacob moved the cursor over to the right. "Someone already put an account number in here. They just wrote a short piece of code to direct you to this website and input the account number for you. All that's needed is the password for it."

"Another password? Try the one that allowed us to access the drive."

Jacob looked at Ben's ID card and typed in the digits. The website returned *PASSWORD NOT A MATCH FOR THIS ACCOUNT.*

"Why give me this if I don't know the—" Ben stopped. *Think. Think about it.*

He reached for the keyboard and slowly typed in nine digits, considering each one.

A new page came up immediately. All three stared in silence at the figure at the bottom of the page.

"This account has close to $600 million in it," Jacob said softly. He turned suddenly. "What was your password?"

"My social—my social security number—backwards. That's the reason for that whole 'socially backward' nonsense."

Yuri whistled. "What do you intend to do with this?"

Ben stared hard at the computer screen. What to do indeed.

"This much money, I'm sure there is someone else looking for it. Matter of fact, I *know* someone is. Did Dad ever mention a man named Stephen to you, Yuri?"

Yuri's face twisted. "Yes. He talked about him but I never met him. From what I was told, not a good man. Why?"

"I was followed when I left North Carolina and come to find out it was him who set it up. I suspect there are still people watching what I do. He hasn't made any overt moves yet but I bet he's planning something. Just don't know what yet." Ben turned back to Jacob. "Any way I can talk you into doing a little creative programming for me? I need some safeguards put on this money."

Jacob smiled, the first one Ben had seen cross his face. "I believe you can afford it."

⟞⟝

The Camaro rolled to a stop at the end of the street. It didn't look out of place here—there were two others parked in front of other houses. One was being washed by a man who was clearly comfortable in his own skin, due to the amount of it he was currently displaying. As Billy watched, the man shouted something toward his house. A younger, thinner version of the man came out with a beer in his hand and gave it to the car washer. The man drank half of the beer and continued spraying the Camaro.

"Whose house is that?" Danny asked.

"Not sure. We'll let Colin know the address and they can figure it out."

"You think he spotted us coming up here?"

Billy considered this. There had been several times in the last two weeks that he was certain they had been made, but Ben had done nothing to indicate he was any wiser. It was hard to tell with some of these soldier boys. Some were smart, others not so much.

"We'll just have to wait and see."

Billy picked up his phone, found Colin's number, and hit dial.

⊷ ⊶

"Stephen, we have news."

Stephen came into the dingy living room and sat on the sofa. He made a disgusted face as dust flew up, then sighed. "What is it?"

"Benjamin finally left Black Creek and came here to Memphis. Billy and his boys have eyes on him over in East Memphis."

Stephen considered this for a moment. "Do they know who he's visiting?"

"No, they only have an address."

Stephen gestured impatiently. "Go on, then, look it up. Do your Internet thing."

After a few clicks, Colin said, "According to this, a man named Yuri Shevchenko lives at that address with his son Jacob."

"Yuri Shevchenko?" Stephen thought for a moment. The name sounded familiar. He made a decision.

"Tell Billy to back off and keep an eye on Benjamin. I believe the Russians can handle Yuri." He paused, thinking. "Okay. Let's speed this up. I vaguely remember this man Yuri; I know that William dealt with him a few times, even assisted him in getting here to the States. Benjamin wouldn't visit him without a reason. While the Russians deal with Yuri, we will go have a talk with Billy and his men."

CHAPTER TWENTY-ONE

"What's on your mind?"

Karen didn't want to seem like she was prying, but it was obvious to her that something was bothering Ben.

"I finally went to find out what's on this drive I told you about," he said. "Now I kind of wish I hadn't bothered."

There was pizza on the coffee table, and Karen pulled another piece from the box. It was nice to be with someone who didn't expect her to cook all the time. Pizza is a lot easier to clean up, too.

Before she took a bite, she asked, "Why? What did you find out?"

Ben sighed. "So, this is all tied up with what I told you about my dad. I told you about how I got it, how I've just kept it all these years. Today I went to Memphis to see a man about helping me with it. Turns out there's a ton of money out there and this thing is the key to getting it."

"What? Did your dad leave you an inheritance or something?" she asked through a bite of pizza.

"Sort of. Except it's close to $600 million worth."

Karen coughed up the bite she had just taken. She turned and looked at Ben, wide eyed. She coughed again, then grabbed her glass of water to take a drink. Ben watched her, amused.

"Huh. You're even cute when you're choking."

"Shut up. Did you say 600 *million?*"

"Yes. That much." He looked at the wall and took a drink of his beer. "You know, I've had some friends tell me stories about inheritances where the family got together and argued about who was getting what. I can just imagine how much of a fight this much would cause."

"Ben, that's the kind of money someone would kill for. Not even joking. Did you get any of it?"

"Not yet. Yuri—that's the man in Memphis I went to see—his son, Jacob, is good with programming. I had him set some security in place, in addition to what's already there. The last couple of weeks, there have been some guys keeping an eye on me, I'm sure of it. I have a feeling Stephen is going to try to get at it before too long."

"So…what are you going to do?"

He looked at her. "I'm working on it. You must know that he knows we're together, and I wouldn't put it past him to try to do something to you just for some leverage. How is KC's for security, anyway?"

"There's a Mossberg pump under the bar, and I keep a Sig in my office in the back. Have you told the sheriff? Does he know about any of this?"

"Not yet. How is Jamie doing? He used to be in the infantry; I think he'll be all right if anything goes down."

"He's doing fine, especially now that he asked Jen out." She smiled. "You should see the two of them. They're pretty cute together."

"I'm sure they are. Back to the potential violence part, though… how many others do you have working there?"

"Jamie Jen and Bobby are full time—you know Bobby; he's the cook in the back. Stacy and Michelle on the weekends. That's it. Two of the deputies, Mark and Carl, I pay them for extra security when they aren't on duty and I'm expecting a crowd. That's it."

⚊+ +⚊

The two reclined in Karen's bed. "Tell me about your ex wife," she said.

Ben started a little at this. From what he had been told by others, whenever a current mate asked about previous ones, it usually led to an argument, hurt feelings, bad language, and so on. He knew he was developing strong feelings for Karen; he had no idea that something like this would occur so early.

They had been together for two weeks now. The relationship was gaining strength every day—when he wasn't working on his mother's house, he was helping her at KCs. They had finished up at the bar and decided to have dinner together. The next thing he knew they were kissing on the couch, and that led to her bedroom. Ben tried to remember who had initiated it, but that was a trivial thought—he didn't really care, as he lost himself in her embrace.

It made sense for her to ask about Lauren, he supposed—his mother had told Karen that he had been married, and he knew that his mother had pictures of the two of them.

Minefield. I should step carefully with this one. This was a blissful moment, the two of them together.

Don't fuck this up, he thought.

"What would you like to know?"

Karen considered the question. She was lying on his outstretched arm as she thought. Ben wanted to move it as it was going to sleep but he didn't want to ruin the moment.

"I've seen pictures of the two of you at your mother's house, and you looked happy in them," she said. "Believe me, I know that

153

pictures don't always tell the whole story. Your mother told me you two were having problems. I was just wondering what happened." She propped herself up on her elbow so she could look in his eyes. "You don't have to talk about her if you don't want to."

A way out of the minefield! No, wait—could be a trap. She had initiated this conversation, so Ben felt obligated to continue. *Besides*, he admitted to himself, *I want her to know*. He was falling hard for her, and he did not want to screw this up.

"We met when I was posted to Fort Bragg. A friend of mine introduced us at a bar up in Raleigh. She was going to school up at the University of North Carolina to be a doctor.

"At first she thought it was pretty cool; she had never been around military guys. She loved the uniform, hearing the stories about jumping out of airplanes, all that. Her parents weren't real crazy about me, thought that she could do better than a soldier. This was all before September 11, before everyone in a uniform automatically became a hero. I tried to win her folks over, and I think her dad eventually warmed up a little but her mom absolutely hated me.

"She did her internship at the VA in Fayetteville after she graduated. She was really into helping the vets, you know? I could tell, though, that seeing a lot of how they were treated was starting to affect her. Little things—she would come home crying about one vet or another, how they were basically just dropped off by their families and left to die. She heard all kinds of stories there—in the late '90s, there were still a lot of World War II and Korean veterans around."

Ben paused. "Funny thing, too—you would think that being around them would have prepared her for what was happening in our marriage. I came back from my first trip to Afghanistan and I was trying to deal with it. We trained and trained and I admit I was thrilled to get into the fight. She thought I was an idiot—why was I so excited to get into combat? She dealt daily with old men who had seen it and she saw how it affected them. Why would I want to do something like that?

"I couldn't explain it to her. I was finally going to get in the game, and when I got home all I wanted was to be left the hell alone. She tried her best to understand but I could tell it was frustrating for her."

He laughed. "This was 2002. I was outside the wire the entire deployment, getting shot at and shooting back. After six months of this, I was exhausted and ready to come home. I remember getting back to Bagram and getting all the redeployment briefs—I'm sure you remember those too—and the one thing that absolutely blew my mind was how much emphasis the Army put on not going home and beating your spouse. A shit ton of briefings on how hard it had been on our *families* but very little on how *I* was supposed to deal with coming back to civilization. Isn't that crazy?"

Karen nodded. "I remember those too. There had been a lot of incidents where guys came back and started abusing their wives and kids."

Ben nodded. "I'm not saying it wasn't justified. At least the regular Army got some homecoming shit, the families all meeting up at Green Ramp over at Pope Air Force Base when the birds came in. My team got home in the middle of the night and we weren't allowed to even get off the plane for three hours because lightning had struck three miles away. After we turned in our weapons at the arms room, I finally got to go home. I had managed to call Lauren and let her know I was on my way, but of course she was at work that night pulling a double shift.

"I'm whining. I know. I chose to volunteer for the unit I was in, and I loved being there. All of this *does* play into why we ended up divorced, though.

"After my third trip down range, I knew. I knew our marriage was done and...honestly, by that point I no longer gave a shit. Every time I got ready to go she found some excuse to not see me off—work, her parents, something. Like I said, I no longer cared. She was—still is—a good person. She just didn't know how to deal with me anymore. I was drinking too much, sobering up just long enough to get to work every day, and then hitting it again in the evening. I never hit her or abused her, never wanted to. I just no longer cared.

"We got divorced in 2007. As far as I know, she still lives there in Fayetteville. When we saw an attorney, she said she wanted no alimony, she just wanted it over. She was getting ready to start her own practice so I wondered if she was thinking I wanted alimony from *her*. I made it clear I was also done. I don't recall much of the discussion because I'm pretty sure I was drunk for the whole thing."

He looked at the ceiling for a moment and then looked at Karen again. "That's pretty much it. I did love her, if that's what you were wondering, but I ain't carrying a torch anymore. She's part of my old life. I hate to admit part of the bad times."

Karen traced a circle on his chest. "I get it. Here's my other question—why did you stay in so long if you were having so many problems?"

"Honestly? It was all I had. Oh, I told lots of people that I hated being down range, getting shot at, sleeping on rocks and worrying about dying, but I knew that I *liked* it. I can imagine that most people have no idea of what it means to really be alive. *Really* alive. You know what I mean, don't you?"

Karen made a non-committal sound. "I guess. I wasn't over there as long as you were and that one time was plenty enough for me. I don't want to worry about dying."

"I decided to retire because my body was wearing out more than anything, and I saw my future as a senior guy—meetings, meetings, emails, meetings, not being out front, and meetings. Did I mention I hate meetings?"

Karen laughed. "I think I figured that one out."

CHAPTER TWENTY-TWO

Reggie called Ben the next day and asked if he wanted to take a ride. Ben couldn't refuse—he enjoyed being around his old friend, and after learning more about the developing situation, he wanted to fill Reggie in.

Reggie was in high spirits as they drove, and the conversation turned to people they both knew.

"You know the McCullars, lived out near the lake?" Reggie asked.

"Yeah, I remember them."

"So, the youngest, Phillip Joseph—everybody just calls him PJ 'cause that name sounds kind of, I don't know, highborn... That dumbass hijacked a CVS truck not long ago."

Ben sipped his coffee. "Okay, so what?"

"Well," Reggie continued, "he and another one of the local idiots figured they could get a bunch of Sudafed so they could go into the meth cookin' business and make themselves some money. There were two problems with their little scheme, though: the trucking companies all track their trucks with GPS these days and the truck they hijacked contained nothing but a shipment of lady goods and aspirin."

"Huh."

"Yep. Hard to cook meth with tampons and whatnot. They pulled the truck off Route 34 next to an old farmhouse about ten miles from the interstate, cut the locks, and found out they had jack shit. Funny thing, too—the driver just straight let them have the truck when they put a gun in his face, waited for them to pull away, and called the police as soon as the truck was out of sight."

"Nice. What happened to them?"

Reggie laughed. "Oh, they got put away. The judge, no shit, actually used the words 'dumbass' and 'moronic' in his courtroom."

Reggie reached down to the radio and pulled the mike from its holder. He keyed it and spoke. "Dispatch? You there?"

Reggie frowned when there was no response. "Damn it, I wonder if this thing's broken. It's been awful quiet."

Ben took another sip of his coffee and pulled out his phone. "You shouldn't have any problems around here, right? I mean, we aren't that far out. Let me see if I can call your office."

Ben turned his phone on and looked at the screen. *NO SERVICE* was at the top.

He grunted. "That's weird."

"What?"

"I know we're in Mississippi and all, but I can't remember the last time I had no service at all, even running around some of these back roads."

A cold feeling settled into Ben's stomach.

He looked at Reggie. "Give me your phone. Who's your carrier?"

"Mid-South Communications. Why? What are you thinking?"

"Just give me your phone."

Reggie plucked it from his pocket and handed it to Ben. Ben looked at the screen and saw the same message that there was no service. "Shit. Do you have a radio on you?"

Reggie frowned. "No, we had to send a couple back for repair so I gave the working ones to the deputies. I knew I would be in the car all day..." He took his eyes from the road and gave Ben a serious look. "What the hell is going on right now?"

"I'm not sure at the moment but I think...hey, what's that?"

Reggie turned his gaze back to the road.

A hundred yards to their front on the right side of the road an old Ford pickup was sitting with the hood up. Ben saw a younger man sitting in the driver's seat and another man partially hidden by the raised hood. As Reggie slowed the vehicle, Ben saw the younger man watching the rear view mirror. The man at the front of the truck dropped out of sight around the hood and moved to the passenger side.

The cold feeling hadn't left Ben's stomach. For some reason he couldn't identify, this seemed wrong.

"Drive on by; don't stop. Turn your lights on if you have to, but don't stop."

Reggie's eyes were narrowed as he looked at the truck, but he said, "I have to, man, I'm the sheriff. If these guys are in trouble and I don't stop, I'll never hear the end of it from the folks around here."

Ben knew this part of the county well, often taking this road to avoid the law when he was young and drinking. There wasn't a house for three miles in either direction. The most traffic this road saw was teenagers, drunks, and farmers driving their tractors from one area to another.

In other words, if you really wanted to ambush someone...

Ben made his decision. It was difficult due to the equipment in the patrol car, but he maneuvered his left leg around the center console and jammed his foot on top of Reggie's, pressing the accelerator to the floor. "DRIVE!"

Reggie was surprised by Ben's move and the sudden burst of speed from the car. He jerked the steering wheel to the left to avoid hitting the parked truck. "What the HELL—"

His shout was interrupted by glass shattering and what sounded like angry bees flying through the car.

"They're shooting at us!" Ben shouted.

A round punched through the headrest on Ben's seat. This saved the sheriff's life as it had been traveling directly for the side of his head. Instead, it clipped Reggie's forehead just above his right eyebrow. Reggie's head rocked back and blood immediately ran into his right eye.

"Jesus Christ!" He fought to maintain control of the speeding car.

Ben's instincts took over. He yanked his foot back and grabbed the pistol he had at the small of his back. He spun in the seat and rapidly emptied his magazine at the receding truck. He ducked down in the seat to retrieve another and looked at Reggie.

"Shit, you took one."

Reggie grimaced as he watched the road. "Just skimmed me." He ran his sleeve across his forehead and angrily looked at the fresh blood. "How in the hell did you know that was going to happen?"

Ben let out a nervous laugh as he replaced the empty magazine in his pistol. "My neck hairs were standing up. How far are we from your house?"

"My house? Fuck my house! I'm getting back to the station and rounding up every damn deputy I can."

"We're closer to your house than we are to town, brother. I have a feeling all this shit is going down for a reason. That was an *ambush*, not just two rednecks shooting at the sheriff. No comms? Two guys knowing what route we were traveling and *ready* for us? Come on, man. That was a little too convenient."

Reggie whipped his head around to look at Ben. Blood flew from his face and landed on the console between them. "What the *fuck* have you gotten me into?"

Ben didn't want to look at his oldest friend. He knew that all of this had to do with him.

"Look brother, I'm going to make this right. First, though, we need comms. You have a landline at your house, right?"

Reggie concentrated on the road. "Yes. Linda wanted us to always have something other than cell."

Ben had another gut feeling. He thought for a second, and then decided. "Those boys were intent on hitting us, but they didn't seem like they were really trying to *kill* us, wouldn't you say?"

"I have no idea. I've never been ambushed on a country road before in my own goddamn county. Seems to me like they were trying to kill us."

Ben shook his head. "There was a lot of lead in the air but except for a couple of rounds that went through here, it doesn't look to me like they were going for a kill." He considered what this meant. "I think they were just trying to scare us and herd us somewhere…"

"Well, they damn sure scared the shit out of me. My house is coming up in about a mile."

"Okay, wait." Ben couldn't explain it, but he knew that if this was a setup there were more surprises in store. "Pull up just shy of your driveway, just next to those trees where the car can't be seen."

"What…wait. What the hell are you wanting to do now? I'm going to my house to make a call and get some backup. We're going to wait it out right there in my house with every gun I can put my hands on."

"Man, please listen to me. I told you I'm going to make this right. Trust me. I think I've seen this before, okay? Didn't I tell you to keep driving because we were going to be ambushed?" Ben pleaded.

Reggie's face was a mask of hurt, rage, and fear. He pulled over where Ben had instructed.

"I know you did a lot of things in the Army. I can't even imagine the shit you know, the shit you've seen, the shit you know how to do. I need you to remember something, though—that ain't you anymore."

"I know man, I just—"

"Stop. I'm going to trust you on this one because I know I'm out of my element here. My instinct is to get help, as much of it as I can, as much as the law will give me. I *will* bring these assholes in, but it looks like I'm dealing with something different this time and I ain't too big to admit I need help. Now, what is it you want me to do?"

Ben drew a deep breath. "Go to your house. Don't go directly up the driveway either; I think there may be somebody there waiting. Make the calls, hell, call *everybody*. I'm going to take your car and draw those guys off, if you let me."

Reggie nodded. "In any other circumstances, I wouldn't do this. You aren't an officer of the law. I *better* get my car back."

⊶⊷

Reggie watched as Ben spun the cruiser in a tight circle and drove rapidly back the way they had traveled. He drew his pistol from the holster on his belt and moved toward his house through the woods.

His mind raced. Nothing like this had ever happened to him, in all his years of being in law enforcement. Except for that one time so many years ago on a dirty street in Memphis, he had not used his sidearm. He hadn't even drawn it in the line of duty since then, which was one of the attractions of being a rural Mississippi sheriff—most of his time was spent coordinating others. He had plenty of young men and women who were gunfighters; he had no reason to look for a fight. Reggie truly believed in keeping the *peace*—wasn't that why they called them peace officers?

He approached the ancient oak that was the centerpiece of his front yard and peered around it at his front door. His eyes moved across the porch, looking for anything out of place. The garage door was closed, —that was normal. Maybe Linda was still in town or had driven back to Oxford. That gave him a little hope—*Please God, I don't want her here right now.*

He moved at a low crouch to his porch, wincing as the second step made a loud creaking sound. Damn it, another one of those *I'll get around to it* jobs he had been meaning to complete. He eased himself to the front door and tried to look inside, but the curtains were closed. Drawing a deep breath, he grasped the knob on the front door and turned it.

He expected resistance, indicating Linda had locked it, yet the door swung open. The front hall was dark, but light spilled into the living room from the kitchen.

"Baby? Linda? Are you here?"

"I'm in the kitchen," a shaky reply came back.

Reggie didn't notice the tremor in her voice. The adrenaline was pounding through his skull and caused him to miss a telltale sign that everything was not okay.

He breathed a sigh of relief and holstered his pistol. He shut the door behind him and rushed through the living room.

"Baby, you are *not* going to believe—"

He stopped and dropped his hand back on the butt of his side-arm when he saw his wife. Her eyes were teary and huge, and there was a darkening bruise on her left cheek. She sat rigidly at the table, her hands tied in front of her.

His thumb had begun to unsnap the retention strap on his holstered weapon when a high-pitched voice said, "I wouldn't if I was you, Sheriff."

CHAPTER TWENTY-THREE

B en gripped the steering wheel tightly. His ears still rang from unloading a full magazine at the attackers and a stage ten headache was brewing. He fought myopia, the urge to focus only on the road ahead in his search for the ones who had brought this pain.

Stephen. Has to be. First, he hires a complete crew of idiots to watch my every move and then acts on what he hears. Ben was aware of the tactic, having seen it played out dozens of times. Gather intelligence, make a plan, get the players into position, and then execute the plan. The plan in this case being *get the money that Ben had access to.*

He struck the wheel and made a strangled enraged sound. *For fuck's sake—come at* me. *Leave everyone else out of this. I'm tired of people being hurt because of me.*

Ben rounded a curve and almost struck the old Ford truck barreling the opposite way. A savage grin split his face—*Now you're just dealing with* me. *I know how to react to an ambush, you sons of bitches. When in doubt, counterattack.*

"Shit! That's him! Why's he coming back? And where's the damn sheriff??"

Rick grunted and spun the wheel. The rusty truck squealed in protest but Rick managed to turn the vehicle around and accelerate toward the cruiser that had just screamed past.

"Don't worry about the sheriff," Rick said. "The boys got a surprise for him at his house. We're just supposed to get this one. Get that rifle ready."

Tim brought his rifle up and leaned out the window as the truck gained on the cruiser.

"Shoot his tires out and try not to kill him, jackass. Last time you almost put both of them in the ground. Do I need to remind you what'll happen if we bring him back dead?"

"Fuck off, Rick; I know what I'm doing. Just keep this thing steady so I can aim properly." Tim eased the rifle out of the window and took aim at the patrol car.

⚊⚊

Normally a rust bucket pickup truck wouldn't stand a chance against a standard police car. Two things were in the truck's occupants' favor: the road they were on was extremely curvy, with decades of dense growth crowding both sides and obscuring visibility, and Ben wanted the boys to catch up. His thoughts were to draw them away from Reggie, and lead them to a spot where he had the advantage.

The adrenaline pumped through his system. The anger, the frustration, the fear were still there—but he realized that he had not felt this alive since his last time overseas. Every nerve wide awake, he could smell, hear, see everything. He felt invincible. He was going to take care of this.

He glanced at the rear view mirror and saw the truck gaining. A grim smile appeared on his face, and he looked down to ensure his pistol was ready.

There was one thing that had slipped Ben's mind in all the excitement. If you are alone in a tactical situation like this one, being alone is a severe handicap. Everyone in a vehicle has their assigned role—the driver drives, the gunner guns, the passenger seat occupant maintains communications, and those in the back seat watch their sectors.

What worked most against Ben was that he had to focus on driving. Taking your eyes from the road, even for a few seconds, can have disastrous consequences.

In this case, a split second of inattention was compounded by Tim's bullets finding the rear tire, causing the vehicle to swerve to the side of the road toward several trees. Ben fought to control it but overcorrected, making the rear of the car spin around. The gravel on the shoulder gave no traction to the rear wheels when the vehicle spun 180 degrees, throwing Ben against his seatbelt.

The front of the car slammed into the trees.

The last thing he heard was a loud *BANG* as the air bags deployed.

The Ford came to a stop behind the wrecked cruiser. Rick and Tim got out, Tim still cradling the rifle.

"Watch him, make sure he don't try anything," Tim said.

Rick walked to the driver's side and with a grunt hauled the door open.

"He alive?" Tim asked nervously.

Rick smiled. "Oh yeah, he's alive. Air bag knocked him straight out. We're good."

CHAPTER TWENTY-FOUR

Reggie stood in his kitchen, his face burning with anger. He held his hands up.

"Baby, are you okay?" he said, straining to keep his voice level.

"Oh, she's just *fine*, Sheriff! Come on in and join us!" the man said gleefully, his pistol pointed at Linda's head.

As Reggie eased his way into the kitchen, the man held up his hand. "Real quick, Sheriff, I want you to reach across with your left hand, grab that pistol, and hand it to me butt first. Slow. Nice and slow."

Reggie couldn't take his eyes away from his wife. Hers were wide and brimming with tears, and he felt some of his own welling up. Not from fear, but anger—true, white hot anger. This piece of human garbage was pointing a gun at his wife's head, and there was nothing he could do.

He eyed the bruise on her cheek, the one he had lovingly kissed so many times. The fury roared through his blood, compounding his guilt at not being able to control the situation. He fought valiantly to maintain control. There was no way this man was going to get away with hurting her.

Reggie complied and handed his pistol over. He raised his hands again, palms out, and looked at the man. He looked familiar.

As the man tucked Reggie's pistol into the back of his dirty jeans, he grinned.

"I bet you're wondering where you know me from, ain't you, Sheriff?" The man's grin widened. "My name's Daniel—most folks call me Danny—and you put me away about a year ago. That help any?"

It did. Reggie's anger deepened. "Yes, I remember you," he spat. "You're a convicted rapist, right?"

The grin dropped from Danny's face. "Rapist? That girl was seventeen years old and asking for it! It was a bum deal and you know it!"

Reggie knew he must maintain his composure. He said nothing further to anger Danny.

Danny fumed for a moment, then visibly attempted to calm himself. "That don't matter now, anyways, does it?" The grin reappeared. "The past is past. What matters is right now, huh?" He looked down at Linda, then back at Reggie. He frowned.

"Where's your friend?"

"He took off. Don't know where he went."

Danny laughed. "I bet you were wondering why you had no cell phone coverage or radio, huh? Well, Mr. Sheriff, you ought to check your car more often. There's a cell jammer under the right rear fender and *somehow*"—his eyes widened comically—"the cable going to the radio antenna on the roof got cut. Need to be more careful in the future."

Reggie grimaced. Rookie mistake, not checking everything daily.

"Yeah, I was scared you might notice it but since that fellow Ben got back, you ain't been paying a lot of attention to anything," Danny continued. "Speaking of the future, though: If you want to have one, you are going to sit your ass down and stay quiet."

Reggie took a seat at the table.

"Now take your cuffs and put them on," Danny instructed.

As Reggie was complying, he heard a flush from the bathroom in the rear of the house.

Danny rolled his eyes and shouted, "Ain't you done yet?"

"Shut the fuck up," a voice came from behind the door of the bathroom.

Danny shook his head. "That's my cousin Patrick. I don't think that boy can go two hours without taking a shit."

A smell wafted into the kitchen, a smell Reggie knew too well.

"God *dammit* Pat! Are you blazing up *again*?" Danny said, disgusted. "Another thing that boy can't go any time without."

Danny turned and faced Reggie. He sighed. "Okay, Sheriff, this is how it's going to go. We are going to sit here until I get a call. After I do, we're all going to load up in that nice car you got in the garage and head out south of town near the ball fields. My boss is really interested in talking to you."

Reggie, his hands cuffed in front of him, asked, "So who's your boss? Why are you doing this? You have to know this isn't going to end well for you, kidnapping the sheriff."

Danny's smile showed teeth that hadn't seen a toothbrush in a long time. "Funny thing about money, Sheriff. It makes a lot of things turn out okay."

CHAPTER TWENTY-FIVE

Was there anything finer than an Escalade?

Anton loved driving it. He liked the way it handled—a larger vehicle that drove like a car. He shined the glossy black exterior daily, never allowed anyone to even think of eating inside. The last time one of the boys had attempted to light a cigarette while sitting in the passenger seat, Anton had driven his right fist into the man's jaw. He did so without taking his eyes from the road. From that point forward, no one dared do anything in the vehicle without asking permission first.

Except Joseph. The boss' son. Little prick had no respect for anything.

Anton knew his role. As one of the few men in Dmitri's crew who had lived in Russia, he was aware of how good he had it here in the United States. These other boys, they knew nothing of true hunger, of having to fight for anything and everything. Anton and Sergei had accompanied Dmitri to the US, had protected him, and in return Dmitri gave them everything they needed.

Unfortunately, blood really is thicker than water and Anton had to tolerate the idiot Joseph just because he was the heir.

Anton navigated the Escalade into the driveway of Sergei's house.

"How do we know this Yuri?" Anton asked in his stilted English as he took a seat in Sergei's living room.

"Dmitri told me he was with the KGB," Sergei answered, sipping his drink. "He is Ukrainian."

Anton grunted. "And what do we want with him? What are we to do?"

Sergei smiled. "The man Stephen is so obsessed with paid a visit to Yuri just the other day. Evidently Yuri knows something or is helping this man. We need to find out what they talked about."

"Fine. The man was KGB so he should be used to unpleasantness. Do you want me to go alone or take some of your...help?"

Sergei knew Anton was not fond of most of his crew, felt they were too young and inexperienced to really be of any use. He wanted to remind Anton that he himself had been young once, but when Anton was younger he was living in Russia where the rules were different. Being able to take a beating and keep your mouth shut were base rules for life in Russian gangs at that time, and Anton had a feeling that these younger ones could do neither. Sergei agreed with him, to a point. The problem was there were no others who were even willing to get their hands dirty.

"Take Gregory and Philip. They're the most reliable of the ones I have right now."

Anton grunted again. "They will do. And Joseph...?"

Sergei did not hesitate this time. "Absolutely not. Dmitri was adamant that his son not be involved with any of this business. He is not to take any part."

Anton laughed. "So…is the boss concerned about his son's safety, or worried that he will fuck everything up?"

Sergei smiled and nodded. "A little of both, I believe."

———

Three young men waited at the table outside of a trendy bistro just around the corner from Beale Street.

Gregory and Phillip sat across from Joseph eating fried calamari. They watched in distaste as he crammed them into his mouth and spoke around a mouthful.

"What is the plan for tonight, boys? Huh? We're going after some bitches, right?"

Gregory made a face as he wiped away a bit of food that had landed on his shirt. "Sure, Joseph. Whatever you like."

Gregory and Philip didn't care for Joseph in the least. They tolerated him for one reason—he was the boss' son. They resented being saddled with him, but Sergei had made it clear on numerous occasions that they were responsible for keeping him out of trouble.

"I have some on Facebook that I'm talking to right now," Joseph said. "I'm sure tonight will be a good time!"

Gregory looked at Philip and rolled his eyes. He was careful to ensure Joseph didn't see it—Joseph had an annoying habit of seeing everything done in his presence as a potential insult. The amount of cocaine he snorted daily contributed to his overly sensitive nature by making him paranoid, manic, and a general pain in the ass.

———

Anton pulled the Escalade up to the curb next to the three. He scowled when he saw Joseph. He'd hoped Joseph wasn't with the other two. Now there could be an issue.

Gregory watched Anton as he parked, then turned and looked at Philip. He cut his eyes at the Escalade in a nonverbal signal to go.

Joseph looked up from his phone and noticed the two getting up. "Where are you going? I thought we were hanging out."

Philip glanced at Joseph. "We have business, Joseph. We'll see you later."

Joseph stood. "Business? Where? I want to go with you."

Philip tried to suppress a grin. "I'm sorry, Joseph, but you aren't allowed to go on this one. Keep talking to your bitches."

Joseph's thin face grew dark. He stood, almost knocking his chair over. "*You* don't get to tell me what to do, Philip. Or you, Greg. I will call my father and let him know how I am being treated by you."

It was Gregory's turn to laugh. "Joseph, who do you think told us you were not to come along? Hmm? The boss said you cannot go. That's that. Go home. Get ready for tonight! We won't be long!" He continued laughing as the pair got into the vehicle and shut the doors.

Fuming, Joseph stood there, watching the Escalade pull away. He looked around and noticed a taxi sitting across the street. He ran over to it and leaned in the window.

The young black man in the driver's seat looked up. "You need a ride, man?"

"I will give you $500 to take me where that Escalade is going. If you lose them, you get nothing. Understand?" Joseph waved a roll of bills at the driver.

The driver took one look at the money and said, "Get in."

⊶⊷

Joseph watched furtively as the driver followed the three in the huge SUV. His anger continued to intensify. How dare they leave him out? Didn't they realize who would be in charge when his father passed on?

He knew they had no respect for him, considered him a child. He would show them what this *child* could do. He was shaking with fury at the insult. Rather than attempt to calm down, he decided he needed more encouragement for the showdown he was envisioning. He felt in his jacket pocket for the vial, retrieved it and spun the top. On his key ring was a tiny spoon. He filled the spoon with the powder from the vial and carefully snorted it. He closed his eyes and leaned back.

Everything in the universe suddenly clarified. The Memphis sun was blazing through the windshield, twinkling on the windshields of a thousand other cars. He narrowed his eyes against the blaze, feeling his courage amp to the maximum. A giggle escaped his lips as he pocketed the vial and touched under his left armpit, reassuring himself that the pistol was still there.

The taxi driver had skillfully followed the Escalade as it wound its way through downtown Memphis.

"Go one more block and pull over. There. Pull over there," Joseph instructed the driver.

Satisfied, Joseph handed the driver five $100 bills. He held up three more, and with a quick sniffle told him, "This is to forget my face. Understand?"

The driver was more than understanding. Forget a skinny white boy who obviously had a gun under his jacket and snorted coke in his cab? Done and done. Once Joseph had shut the door behind him, the driver took off.

—⟨+ +⟩—

Anton had noticed the taxi. It was his job to be paranoid about everything.

Gregory and Philip were checking their pistols. Anton admitted to himself that weapons were necessary in this line of work, but to question an old man? Even one who had been in the KGB. Carrying weapons was a good way to have additional charges brought against you even if they were never used.

Parked next to the curb, he turned to the boys in the back and said, "Okay, you know the plan. Sergei just needs information, that's all. Remember, he is old, but at one time he was KGB so do not underestimate him. Find out what he knows and then we will leave. Understand?"

The boys nodded. *Good*, Anton thought. *No posturing, no bragging, they were just going to do the job.* They got out of the Escalade and walked to the house.

⊷ ⊶

Joseph crouched behind some bushes that shielded him. He watched Gregory and Philip get out and walk to the house. The hedges blocked the view from the street, so he moved behind them toward Yuri's house, being careful to keep them between him and the SUV.

His heart raced and he found it difficult to breathe. The cocaine was screaming through his system. He forced himself to focus, watching Anton. The windows on the SUV were tinted, but not overly so—the morning sun allowed a dim view into the interior, so Joseph could at least see the shape of Anton's head and which way he was looking. He waited for Anton to look the other way so he could make his move.

⊷ ⊶

Yuri looked through the window at the side of his door. He sighed— he knew this was going to happen eventually. He opened the door to the two young men on his porch and stood there, mute. He was not going to initiate anything.

The pair smiled in unison. "Mr. Shevchenko? Hello, sir. May we speak with you?" Gregory said.

"About what?" Yuri said. His expression didn't change.

"We work for Dmitri Ibragimov. He has directed us to discuss certain matters with you, sir," Philip said. "Are you familiar with Mr. Ibragimov?"

Yuri snorted derisively. As if any Eastern European or Russian immigrant in Memphis wasn't aware of him. "I am. What do you wish to discuss?"

"May we come in? We believe these matters are better discussed away from others," Philip said, still smiling.

Punks trying to act tough. Yuri was very familiar with the type, having been one himself long ago. He stepped back from the door and swept his hand briskly to indicate they could enter.

Once they were inside, Yuri shut the door behind them, noting the large black SUV on the street, not quite in front of his house. That was smart—don't park directly in front of a house you may have to leave in a hurry so witnesses couldn't pinpoint which house you were in.

Yuri waved at the sofa as he took his seat facing them.

"What do you want?"

Gregory and Philip wasted no time. "Our superiors noticed that you had a visitor not too long ago. We merely wish to know more about him and what you discussed," Gregory began. "They feel it may have bearing on some of our business arrangements."

Yuri laughed. "I seriously doubt that your...*superiors*...are simply interested in who visits an old man like me. I know Dmitri, your boss. I was one of the agents who helped put him in the gulag."

Gregory and Philip looked at each other in surprise. Yuri chuckled to himself—amateurs. *They will learn in time not to let anything affect their composure when interrogating someone.*

Gregory looked back at Yuri. "Very well, then, Yuri. Let's get to the point, then—we know a man named Benjamin Martin came to see you. We want to know what you talked about, and you are going to tell us."

⚔

Jacob listened through his bedroom door. These were the Russians his father had warned him about, the ones who would more than likely be showing up on their doorstep after they talked to Ben. It sounded like his father had no fear of them. *Why had he let them in?* he thought. *Why not just send them away?*

He went to his closet, being careful not to make any noise. In the very back, covered with clothes, was a double-barreled shotgun his father had given him as a young man. Jacob had only fired it once—he didn't like guns, and he had no desire to hunt—but he still had it loaded because, well, this is Memphis. He pulled it out from the closet and held it close to his chest as he moved back to the door. They were not going to hurt his father.

⚔

Anton continued watching the street. He chided himself—why had he not noticed that this was a cul-de-sac? There was a sign at the beginning of the street that said *NO OUTLET.* He was currently parked facing the cul-de-sac, and if anything happened where he would need to leave in a hurry he would have to either perform a four-point turn or go all the way to the end to turn around.

Damn it. He had paid so much attention to that taxi following them that his situational awareness had slipped. He turned his head—most of the houses on this street appeared unoccupied at this time of day, and several were for sale, indicating no occupants. No one to notice, that was good.

177

Fine. He made his decision: He would turn the vehicle around to face back the way they had come. He looked over his left shoulder to ensure no one was approaching, then put the Escalade in drive.

⊨⊣ ⊢⊨

Joseph couldn't believe his luck. For some reason, Anton was going to drive away, leaving the front of the house unobserved. What an opening!

They don't want me here. It's time to show everyone how useful I can be. Ha! After I take care of…well, whatever this is, they won't have a choice but to respect me, he thought.

Gathering his courage, he moved quickly to Yuri's front porch, opened the door, and walked in.

⊨⊣ ⊢⊨

If Yuri was surprised that he had one more guest, he didn't show it. He was aware of how Russians acted when they wanted something.

Joseph smirked at Gregory and Philip sitting on the sofa. "Hello boys, did you miss me?"

Gregory collected himself first, standing and facing Joseph. "You are not supposed to be here, Joseph."

Joseph waved his hand. "There are many things I am not *supposed* to do, Gregory." He turned to Yuri, who was still not showing any emotion. "Well, old man? Have you told my friends what they want to know?"

Yuri laughed out loud this time. *Russians!* He hated their arrogance, the damnable assuredness that everyone would do as they wanted. He stared at Joseph's smug face and said, "We were getting to it."

Yuri couldn't bear looking at Joseph, so he returned his gaze to the other two.

"You asked about Benjamin. I knew his father, who assisted me in getting out of that Russian shithole I was assigned to. You boys should know—Russia is full of shitholes."

Philip's face grew dark. "Like the Ukraine is a paradise."

"It was until you Russian pigs came in," Yuri shot back.

Gregory held up his hands. "Please. We are not here to discuss relations between our mother countries. We are just here to learn about this Benjamin." He looked at Yuri with what he hoped was an open expression. "Okay?"

CHAPTER TWENTY-SIX

Anton cursed. He noticed movement behind the bushes as soon as he started driving to reposition the vehicle. Too late, he recognized the boss' son as Joseph bounded onto the front porch and entered the house.

He continued to maneuver the Escalade around to the other side of the street, parked, and picked up his phone to call Sergei.

———

Yuri said nothing for a few moments. He maintained a stony expression as he thought about what to tell the three young men.

"As I said, I knew the man's father," Yuri said quietly. "He merely came to visit, to catch up. We talked about his father William for a while, and he left. That's it."

Gregory wanted to maintain control of the conversation before Joseph could ask anything, so he asked, "That's it? There was no mention of money, plans, anything like that?"

Yuri shook his head. "Nothing of the sort. I'm afraid you three have wasted your time. Surely there is something better you can all be doing than questioning an old man, disturbing him in his own home."

Joseph laughed loudly. He focused a bloodshot gaze on Yuri, who saw that his pupils were dilated. "We *know*, old man! We *know*! Stop this bullshitting and tell us what Benjamin said!"

Philip's expression was pained. "Joseph, calm down…" he began.

The pain of being snubbed by Gregory and Philip was roaring in Joseph's head, amplified by the cocaine. The anger at being disrespected by two young men he considered his friends clouded his thinking. He wanted to be done with this seemingly insignificant errand so he could deal with the two of them, to show them who was *truly* the boss. To that end, he made his decision and acted.

He moved his right hand under his jacket and retrieved a shiny pistol. He clicked the safety off and pointed it at Yuri.

In Joseph's mind, his voice was low and threatening, but what emerged from his lips was little more than a squeak.

"Tell us everything or I will kill you."

"*Joseph*—" Gregory shouted.

Yuri's voice didn't waver, nor did his gaze. When he spoke, it was in the same conversational tone he had been using the entire time.

"You little Russian thug. You think this is the first time I have ever had a gun in my face? Pshaw. You are nothing. *Nothing*," he spat.

Jacob's eyes widened as he peered around his door. The man who had burst into his house now had a pistol aimed at his father. He was jittery and sweating profusely.

Jacob closed his eyes, took a deep breath, and moved into the hallway, the shotgun held before him.

Joseph laughed at Yuri.

"Nothing? I am nothing? Old man, do you want those to be your last words?" His knuckles were white where he held the pistol. It wavered slightly as adrenaline mixed with the potent drugs in his system made his hand shake. With his left hand, he wiped sweat from his forehead and leaned closer to Yuri. "I will teach your stupid Ukrainian ass to respect me."

Joseph had been so intent on Yuri that he did not notice Jacob entering the room.

Yuri heard Jacob moving down the hallway and looked in that direction. "Son—" he began, but Joseph wheeled to face Jacob.

"Who are you?" Joseph glanced at the shotgun, his smile widening. "What do you think you're going to do with that?"

Tears ran down Jacob's face as he stopped near Yuri's chair. "You are not going to hurt him." His voice trembled as he spoke.

Joseph looked at Jacob's face. The pistol in his hand had tracked from Yuri to Jacob, and now pointed at Jacob's head.

"That is not your decision to make, pig," and he fired a single round.

Jacob dropped like a puppet with his strings cut.

Yuri roared and launched out of his chair, his face twisted in fury and hate.

Joseph spun back and shot Yuri in his chest. Yuri collapsed back into his chair, the air *whooshing* out of him.

"Jesus *Christ*, Joseph!" Gregory shouted, jumping to his feet from the couch. "What the fuck are you *doing*?"

"You saw them! They were threatening me!" Joseph retorted. He was almost shouting now; the double reports of the pistol made his ears ring. He giggled. "That was louder than I expected! How do people in movies talk normally after something like that?"

Philip was standing now. He shook his head ruefully.

"You fucking idiot, we were only supposed to talk to him, not kill him. What are we going to do now?"

⊰⊹⊱

I'm shot, Yuri thought. *How many times have I been shot now?*

His mind reeled.

My boy, my precious Jacob.

With Herculean effort, Yuri turned his head to look at his son. Jacob's body lay next to the chair, and Yuri let his left hand fall to where he could touch him. There were still tears on Jacob's face.

Yuri only touched Jacob for a second. His mind turned to what he must do next.

He struggled to sit up in his chair and leaned to the right side. There was a numbness in his chest, with a fire building in the center where the bullet had pierced him. He knew he was bleeding out; he knew the bullet had found an artery. His vision was dimming by the second. He had to hurry.

Yuri found the firing device tucked away underneath the chair, next to the bag that held the Chekov mines. He had not moved them recently, so he knew they still faced the three bastards who were arguing with one another. *That's right, you sons of bitches, pay no attention to me.*

He grasped the small green firing device in his hand. It had a simple switch, much like an American Claymore mine. To activate it, all he had to do was squeeze to generate a small electrical charge to the blasting caps inside the mines themselves.

183

He was ready.

He began to cough. He felt blood fly out of his mouth and run down his chin. He fought the cough for a few seconds and tried to draw as deep a breath as he could.

This got the three young men's attention. They stopped arguing and looked at him.

"Damn it, looks like I have to shoot the old bastard again," Joseph said.

"Not necessary," Yuri croaked. The three were now just shadows in Yuri's vision. Yuri forced a smile on his face as he held the firing device up so the three could see it.

"*Dasvidanya,*" Yuri said as he squeezed the device.

━╪ ╪━

"Sergei? Anton. Joseph showed up," Anton muttered into his phone. It had taken several minutes for Sergei to answer, and now Anton was irritated.

"What? How did he get there?" Sergei responded.

"I believe he followed us in a taxi. What should I do?" Anton asked as he watched the front of the house.

Silence on the line.

"Dmitri will not be happy with this," Sergei spoke after a few seconds. "Is there any way you can go in and remove him?"

Anton laughed. "Of course I can, Sergei, but I do not believe the boss would be happy with me for doing what is necessary to remove that idiot."

More silence on the line as Sergei thought. Anton's eyes scanned the street, looking for any more unwanted guests.

Anton's head snapped toward the house. A gunshot. "Sergei, I must go," he said hurriedly. "Someone in there is shooting—" He paused as he heard another shot. "I will call you back."

"Anton, wait—what's happening?" Sergei said, alarmed. "Don't hang up!"

Anton gripped his phone. He opened the door and stepped out of the Escalade. Keeping the phone to his ear, he looked around the neighborhood. No one appeared to be responding to the gunshots. He eased the door shut on the vehicle and began walking toward the house.

"Sergei, I am going in to see what is happening," he spoke into his phone. He paused to check the small of his back for the pistol he kept there.

The pause saved his life. He was only three feet from the vehicle when an explosion blew the door and windows from the front of the house.

The blast knocked him off his feet. He landed on his back, the pistol digging cruelly into his right kidney. Stunned, he dropped the phone, from which Sergei's agitated voice was shouting.

Anton's ears were ringing; he managed to lift his head and look at the house. It was on fire now, but didn't appear to be a tremendous blaze that threatened the neighborhood. In a dazed state, Anton picked up his phone as he got slowly to his feet.

"Anton? *Anton*! What happened?" Sergei shouted. To Anton, his voice sounded far away.

"The house just exploded."

"*What?*" Sergei continued to shout.

"I am coming to you, Sergei," Anton said. "I don't believe anyone is alive in there."

"Yes, get out of there," Sergei instructed. "We will deal with this but we can't if you are in jail."

CHAPTER TWENTY-SEVEN

The building Stephen and Colin were in had been a garage for many years. There had been several owners, and it looked like each one had a serious disregard for hygiene. There was one toilet in the back, and Colin was certain that the last time it had been cleaned was during the Clinton Administration.

The garage had several good points, however: it was isolated from the main road, it was dark, and there were several rusty tools on the benches if they were needed.

Stephen dragged an old plastic chair toward the door and took a seat. "If we haven't heard from them soon, call them."

"Which ones?"

Stephen shot a dark look at Colin. "All of them."

After two and a half weeks of waiting and getting sporadic updates, Stephen had decided to move forward with his plan. After Colin sent word to Sergei to talk to Yuri, he put the other men they hired in motion—two were to find Ben, two went to the sheriff's house, and two went to KC's to get Karen and Jamie. Stephen was happy when Colin told him that Jamie worked for Karen. The other three he had hired were on their way to the garage as they spoke.

"You can use your phone as a Wi-Fi hotspot, right? Do they actually have coverage out here in the sticks?" Stephen asked, gesturing to the laptop on a nearby table.

"Yes, Stephen, everything is ready. All we have to do is wait."

Colin found it strange that Stephen was so anxious. He had counseled Colin numerous times over the years about the necessity of patience, yet now he looked ready to jump at the slightest problem.

Colin's phone trilled. He answered before the first ring stopped.

"Sergei? What is it?"

Colin's face grew ashen as Sergei told him the news. A moment later, he hung up the phone.

He turned to Stephen. "Yuri is dead."

Stephen snorted. "So?"

Colin shook his head. "Dmitri's men are too. That's not the worst of it. His son was there."

Stephen drew a breath. He looked down for a moment, massaging the bridge of his nose. He looked back up.

"His son? That's bad."

"Sergei called only to let me know that Dmitri is currently gathering a few men to come for us so he can discuss the…situation," Colin continued.

Stephen's eyes widened. "Wait. Do they know where we are?"

Colin nodded. "I told Sergei last week that we found this place that's perfect because of its isolation."

"Call everyone. Now," Stephen commanded, getting to his feet. "We have to speed this up."

CHAPTER TWENTY-EIGHT

"Wake up."

The world was dark. Ben could see some light, but it pulsed too much between his half-open eyelids to form any recognizable shapes.

A blast of cold snapped him out of it and the world came into focus. The water that had been thrown in his face ran down to soak his shirt.

Ben's head felt like it was in a vise. He blinked twice, then opened his eyes as much as he could.

"Wake up. Wake the hell up."

The voice was familiar. He turned toward it and Stephen's face came into view.

"Good. I thought those idiots had done permanent damage," Stephen said.

Ben lifted his head as much as he dared, pain blossoming in his skull. He looked around the dark room, trying to regain his senses.

"Stephen, what the hell is going on?" he croaked. He tried to raise his hands to touch his face but they were zip-tied to the arms of the chair he sat in.

Stephen looked down at Ben. "It's simple: I want the money. You have access to it and you are going to give it to me." He smiled. "By the way, in case you were wondering, we didn't do that to you. Those airbags can really do a number, can't they?"

Stephen turned at the sound of a vehicle approaching. The door to the garage opened a moment later and Billy came in shoving Karen and Jamie in front of him. They were also restrained with zip-ties.

Stephen examined Karen and Jamie. Karen had a cut on the left side of her face, and Jamie was limping severely. Stephen eyed Billy and the other man who had followed Billy inside.

"For Christ's sake, are any of them not injured in some way? I'm not against roughing people up, but I gave explicit instructions that they weren't to be harmed. Particularly these two."

Billy shook his head in disgust. "You ain't seen the half of it. We went to get them like you told us. I sent Johnny and Drew here in to bring them out. They was taking too long so I went in to check on things. When I got inside, the woman here had laid Johnny out with a bat and the boy had Drew in a chokehold. Only way I got them off my two boys was to shoot into the ceiling." Billy grimaced. "Even then, the woman was still trying to get at a shotgun behind the damn bar. Next time you tell us to go after somebody, give us a little more heads up that they ain't going quietly."

Stephen grunted. "As much as you and your men are being paid, I would imagine you would take more precautions."

Billy started to reply but Stephen cut him off. "No matter. Colin, call Daniel and have him bring the sheriff here."

⊷⊹⊹⊷

Danny sat at the table, his pistol never leaving Linda's face. He drummed his fingers.

"Damn it, they should have called by now," he mumbled. "PAT! Get the hell out here!"

No reply. The sweet smell of burning cannabis continued to permeate the air.

"For fuck's sake," he groaned, getting up.

He looked at Reggie.

"You do anything stupid, I'll kill her," Danny said, then walked down the hall to the bathroom.

Reggie wasted no time. He reached in his pocket, grabbed his keys, and unlocked the handcuffs. He kept his hands in plain sight, and left the cuffs on his wrists so as not to tip Danny off.

Linda, wide eyed, whispered, "What are you going to do?"

Reggie's face was set in angered determination. "What I have to do. Get ready."

Reggie kept his keys in his left hand, cupping them to keep them out of sight. "Hey!" he yelled. "What's taking so long back there? You idiots are stinking up my damn house!"

Danny came back quickly. His grin had disappeared. Now he aimed the pistol at Reggie.

"Sheriff, are you out of your mind? You ain't running *shit* here. We'll do as we damn well please in your house. Now sit there and keep your mouth shut." Danny turned and faced the hallway. "Pat, you got ten seconds to get your ass out here!"

Reggie readied himself. As Danny turned to face Reggie again, he tossed his keys into Danny's face.

Reggie was counting on the natural reaction someone had when something is flying at their face. It worked. Danny's hands flew up to shield himself, and as he did so, his pistol pointed at the ceiling. Reggie lunged at Danny and tackled him to the floor.

Danny yelled in surprise but reacted quicker than Reggie expected. Snarling, he fought to bring the pistol around to Reggie's face. Reggie grabbed the front of it and yanked as hard as he could while driving the flat of his palm into Danny's nose.

Danny howled in pain as his nose broke. His grip relaxed on the pistol and Reggie pulled it away from him. The sheriff, still holding the pistol by the barrel end, brought the butt down on Danny's forehead. Danny collapsed on the floor.

Pat, hearing all the noise, finally opened the bathroom door. A cloud of smoke billowed around him. He shouted and reached back into the bathroom. He came back out with a sawed-off shotgun, which he pointed in Reggie's direction.

Reggie didn't hesitate. He reversed the pistol in his hand, aimed down the hallway, and fired two rounds.

Pat looked down at the two holes in his shirt, which rapidly filled with blood. He looked up at Reggie, then fell forward.

He didn't make a sound.

Reggie kept the pistol trained on Danny as he got to his feet. It didn't appear Danny was a threat any longer, so he went to the table and put his arms around his wife.

"Are you okay? Did he hurt you?"

Linda was crying now, but her face was furious. "I'm fine. What is happening? Who are they?"

"I'm sorry, sweetie," Reggie replied. "This has to do with Ben." He moved to get a knife and cut her restraints. "He's in trouble, and I have to get him out of it if I can." He got up and moved to the kitchen counter. He picked up the phone and punched in numbers.

"Darren? This is the sheriff. Get all available officers; give the city police a call too. We have a situation."

As he was making the call, Danny's phone rang.

CHAPTER TWENTY-NINE

B en looked at Karen and Jamie. Both were a little roughed up, but the look on their faces was pure fury.

"Holy shit, I'm sorry for getting y'all into this," he said.

Jamie grinned. "Wasn't you, man. If big'un over there hadn't walked in with that gun, I'd still be choking that piece of shit over there." Drew started toward him, and Jamie made a kissing sound in his direction, followed by a wink.

"Stop," Stephen said to Drew. "You'll get your turn. Colin, is Daniel on his way with the sheriff?"

Colin still had his phone to his ear. He sighed. "There's no answer."

Stephen rolled his eyes. "Fine. We'll deal with that later." He turned to Ben. "Down to business. How do you access the account? They use multiple methods for security, and I know you must have something physical. I suspect a thumb drive or something like that."

"In my pocket," Ben said.

Karen and Jamie exchanged a glance. Why was Ben giving it up so easily?

This occurred to Stephen as well. He hesitated, then smiled.

"You're out of time and options, Benjamin. All of this will stop—all the harassment, all the stupidity…once I get what is mine anyway."

Ben's expression didn't change. His look toward Stephen was one of contempt.

"Ain't yours. Wasn't my dad's either, now that I think about it."

Stephen had a hearty laugh at this. "So? So *what*? Do you really think that every single person with money on this earth acquired it honestly? Why do you even care? If I thought you would have gone for it, I would have just called you and said, 'Hey Ben, you have access to a lot of money. I know this, and I am *quite* comfortable with violence, so let's do this: Give me eighty percent of it and I will be on my way. No muss, no fuss. Deal?'"

He squatted in front of Ben. He cocked his head as he examined Ben's features.

"No, that wouldn't work, would it?" he said softly. "I knew I had to have something over you, some leverage. Now you're going to give me all of it."

Ben maintained a steady gaze into Stephen's eyes. Stephen didn't look away.

Finally, Ben said, "It's in my left pocket. Just take it."

Stephen reached into the pocket Ben had indicated and brought out the USB drive. He turned it over thoughtfully.

"This is how you got it out, huh? I never thought to check your magazines," he said. "I looked through everything else. I'm sure you were aware of that."

Ben said nothing.

Stephen straightened, turned and handed the drive to Colin. Colin took the USB and inserted it into the laptop.

Colin bent to the screen and waited. When the drive was accessed, Colin said, "What do I need to do?"

Ben said, "Double click the program icon there; it takes you to the account."

Colin did, then said, "Password?"

Ben tried to sit up. "Undo my hands, Stephen. You have enough artillery in the room, you know I ain't going to do anything."

Stephen considered, then nodded assent. He brought out a knife and cut the restraints that held Ben in the chair. As Ben stood, rubbing his wrists, Stephen said, "Anything stupid, I don't shoot you." He nodded toward Karen and Jamie. "They die first."

Ben nodded and took his wallet from his pocket, pulling out his retired ID card. He leaned over the laptop and typed in the digits.

Colin watched as he did so. The bank webpage accepted the code and displayed the account information. Colin drew a breath, and turned to Stephen.

"It's all there, Stephen. All of it."

Stephen relaxed visibly. "Now we can get to business, Benjamin. You made the right choice. Colin, move the funds to the new account."

Colin roughly pushed Ben away from the computer and began typing. Ben moved away, closer to Karen and Jamie.

Colin frowned. He turned his head to face Stephen.

"There's more security here, Stephen. It says it will not transfer funds without additional authorization and asks for another password."

"Another password?" Stephen said. He looked at Ben and gestured. "Put it in, son. We aren't done yet."

Ben shrugged and moved back to the laptop. He typed in some digits, then grimaced as a warning dialog appeared. "Shit, wait, that ain't it..." He typed again. The dialog reappeared. "Damn it, I know this..."

Stephen's face grew dark. "This had better not be a trick, Benjamin."

"It ain't," Ben said. He looked over at Karen. The look said, *Are you ready if I do something?*

She shot a puzzled look back, one that undeniably warned, *Don't be stupid.*

He offered a small smile. *What do we have to lose?*

Ben suddenly grabbed the laptop and swung it at Colin, hitting him in the face. As Colin recoiled from the attack, Ben swiftly relieved him of the pistol Colin had in a shoulder holster. Ben brought his left arm around Colin's neck and pressed the muzzle of the pistol to the side of Colin's forehead.

Ben's movements were so swift no one reacted for a second. Colin attempted to squirm free but Ben pushed the pistol barrel harder into his temple.

"Just stop," Ben commanded, then looked at Stephen. "Okay, Stephen, this is how it's going to work. You're letting us walk out of here. You ain't getting shit, and if you don't let us go, your boy here dies."

Stephen stood still.

"You have to know you aren't getting out of here alive, Ben."

"I don't think you realize what's going on here, Stephen," Ben said. Without looking at them, Ben said, "Karen, Jamie, y'all get up. Get Stephen's knife and get out of those zip-ties."

As they complied, Ben noticed Billy and the others moving around to try to get a better position. "Stop where you are. Anybody comes any closer, Colin here takes one for the team."

Billy looked at Ben, then said, "Stay where you are, boys." He shot an angry look at Stephen, then at Ben. "For now, anyway."

Stephen regarded Colin, whose face was twisted in anger. Stephen shook his head. "Colin, I'm rather disappointed in you. Fine, Ben, you have us in an impasse. What happens now?" Stephen paused, then said, "Not to sound cruel, but I have to know, did the transfer go through?"

Ben grinned at this. "Good God, Stephen, I have your man here with a gun to his head and you're still wondering about the money? My dad was right about you."

Ben began to move toward the door, being careful to keep Colin between him and the others.

"In a way, it did."

Stephen's eyes didn't leave Ben's as Ben moved. "What does that mean?"

Ben said, "Well, it transferred, but not to any account you have. It's gone from that account you were just looking at, but now it's kind of bouncing around a bit."

"What? What do you mean?"

Ben's grin grew wider as he spoke. "I had Yuri's son Jacob add some security, and if I put the wrong code in a couple of times, the money disbursed to several different accounts I had him set up.

"When I set it up, I tried to think of some worthy causes. Some went to animal charities, some to veteran's groups, homeless shelters, that sort of thing. I gave a couple of LBGTQ charities a million each. Those folks have it kind of rough these days, you know? I mean, it's getting better, but still…"

Ben had read about blood draining from people's faces but had never actually witnessed it before. He did now as Stephen's face turned ashen. Stephen's eyes slowly closed.

"All…all of it? Gone?"

Ben couldn't suppress a smile. "Yep. Gone."

"That don't sound too good," Billy mumbled.

"Jacob can get it back, of course," Ben continued. "Well, a lot of it. I thought you might want to be charitable—all of the donations are in your name, by the way—and I just wanted some insurance, a way to buy time more than anything."

Ben looked around the room, and at Colin.

"In case something like this happened. I didn't know if you had any means of tracking the money anyway. For all I knew, you were just waiting on me to access it, move it, and then I would still be looking over my shoulder for the rest of my life." He stared at Stephen with a mix of sorrow and anger. "All this pain for money, man. I knew I had to draw you out sometime, and I figured it would be best to do it in my own backyard. When y'all are out of the picture that money will go to a good cause, thanks to Jacob."

Colin spoke now, strained due to the pressure Ben was putting around his neck. "You stupid fucking idiot, Jacob is dead."

This shook Ben. "What?"

"The fucking Russians killed him earlier today," Colin said.

Ben was silent at this new development. He began to speak but Billy cut him off.

"Hold on. Let me get this straight. We ain't getting paid?" Billy's deep voice rumbled through the room.

"You'll get paid," Stephen said wearily. "It just may be a little longer. Have patience."

"Patience? Fuck your patience. Me and my boys have broken a shit ton of laws here and we aim to be paid. Paid *well*. That was the deal. Every one of us here is facin' serious damn time for the shit you've had us do over the last couple of weeks."

Stephen turned. "Yes, you are. You also took my money initially on the premise that you would be paid *more* when the job was done. The job isn't done yet. When the job is done, *that* is when you will receive the rest."

He looked at Ben. "You incredibly stupid piece of white trash. You have no idea what you've done."

"Wasn't your money to begin with," Ben said. He was close to the door now, with Karen and Jamie behind him.

Billy pointed his pistol at Ben and Colin. "Y'all ain't going *nowhere*," he snarled. "Me and my boys are going to be paid. We ain't leaving here until we are."

Ben reached the door, and said to Karen, "Get the door open, honey. We're out of here, unless they want Colin here dead. They can sort this all out on their own."

Karen reached for the door, but jumped back as it was thrown open.

Dmitri stood in the doorway, loosely holding a pistol in his left hand.

CHAPTER THIRTY

"It looks like we have interrupted some business," Dmitri said pleasantly. He gazed around the room as three other men came in behind him, each carrying a weapon. One of the men had what appeared to be a machine gun, and placed himself between Dmitri and the others in the room.

Dmitri spoke after a few seconds of silence.

"Stephen? Would you please explain what is happening here?"

"Dmitri, I—" Stephen began, but Dmitri waved his hand.

"Stop. Never mind. It is obvious to me that you do not have matters under control as you should," Dmitri said, gesturing at Ben and Colin.

"Give me a chance to rectify the situation, Dmitri," Stephen said.

Dmitri spoke as if Stephen had said nothing. "Today my son died. Oh, he was a little shit who did nothing right, but he was still my son," he said. "Sergei—you know him—is paying the price for that as we speak. Now my business must go to my daughter, who is away at school in the east. My wife—she is very angry with me. Even though he was a little shit, he was my blood." Dmitri's voice was rising as he spoke. "My *blood*! And that blood is all over a street in eastern Memphis thanks to a fucking Ukrainian that you couldn't take care of yourself."

Dmitri gestured with his pistol. "You told me, Stephen, that everything was under control, that you were going to pay me handsomely for my time and resources. I am assuming that I can at least expect this, yes?"

Stephen drew a breath. "Dmitri, you will get your money, I assure you. It may take longer than I expected."

Ben finally spoke. "Might be a little longer than you think."

Dmitri looked at Ben with curiosity, as if noticing him with a gun to Colin's head for the first time. "Really? *You* are the one who's responsible for all of Stephen's troubles, are you not? You're Benjamin?"

"Mmhmm," Ben responded. "That would be me. Actually, my friends here and I were just on our way out."

Dmitri laughed at this. "I do not believe anyone is leaving."

Billy, who had been silent during all of this, had had enough. He looked around at his boys, nodding at them as they readied their guns.

"Dmitri—Mr. Ibragimov—I have a question for you that Stephen here couldn't answer. Are we getting paid or what?"

Dmitri spun and aimed his pistol at Billy's face. "*You.* You will be quiet until someone addresses you directly, do you understand?"

Billy didn't flinch. "Hell, you think this is the first time I've had a gun in my face? Fuck you, man. If he ain't going to pay us"—he pointed at Stephen—"then you better. We'll be on our way then. I'll tell you this, though: We ain't doing anything until you pay us."

Dmitri didn't drop the pistol as he considered this. He thought for a moment, and appeared to decide. He nodded. "Very well," he said. He turned to the three men who had followed him into the room and spoke rapidly in Russian.

"Dmitri, this isn't necessary," Stephen began. "We can work this out."

Dmitri laughed again. "Give me the money and we leave. Funny, yes? That is the same deal you are being offered by your redneck friend!" He turned and pointed the pistol at Ben and Colin. "You are the one who has access, according to Stephen. Get the money now. I have no desire to stay in this place any longer."

Ben hesitated. "I guess you haven't heard—"

"The money has been moved," Stephen interrupted, talking to Dmitri, "but the only one who could readily access it was the Ukrainian's son who died today. Give me time and I can get it, I promise you."

Dmitri shook his head. "There is a phrase here in America about cutting one's losses, is there not? I have helped you numerous times in the past, Stephen, and you have not always kept your end of the bargain. I kept assisting you because we had similar interests, but it appears you are outliving your usefulness."

Dmitri held his aim at Ben and Colin. "My son is gone. I will be mocked by others if I allow this to continue. How will it look if I let my son's death go unanswered? Hmm?" He shook his head sorrowfully. "I believe it is time to even the playing field," he said, and fired.

The heavy bullet pierced Colin's heart. It exited at an angle and entered Ben's side, striking his ribcage. He shouted at the immediate pain and released Colin to crumple to the floor.

"*COLIN!*" Stephen shouted, and dropped to the floor, drawing his own pistol from underneath his coat.

The Russian who held the machine gun pulled the trigger, and the room filled with its roar. The other two started firing with their own rifles, and the room exploded with even more sound. Three of Billy's men fell as bullets tore through them.

Dmitri turned and fired at Stephen. One bullet went through Stephen's left arm and another shattered his left clavicle.

Stephen clenched his teeth at the pain as he brought his own pistol to bear on Dmitri. He shot Dmitri four times in the chest and watched as Dmitri staggered back against one of the workbenches. Dmitri laughed as he tried to aim at Stephen again.

"Body armor," Dmitri spat.

Stephen adjusted his aim and blew away Dmitri's kneecaps.

Dmitri fell to the floor, his face a mask of pain.

"Fuck you, Stephen," he hissed through clenched teeth.

Stephen responded by firing one round into Dmitri's face.

Billy couldn't believe this. He knew the Russians were insane, but *this*? Jesus!

When the Russian with the machine gun began firing, Billy moved as fast as he could to cover behind one of the support beams in the garage. He watched helplessly as the men he had hired were slaughtered by the high rate of fire from the machine gun. He aimed his shotgun at the machine gunner and fired.

Normally, a shotgun against a machine gun is almost useless, but in the confined space of the garage it worked well. Billy saw the machine gunner's chest cave in as the shotgun blast caught him completely.

Billy pumped the action and fired again at the Russian next to him with similar results.

The last Russian, halfway through reloading, moved quickly to find a way out of Billy's fire.

Karen reached out to Ben as he fell and pulled him away from Colin's lifeless body.

"You're hit!" she exclaimed.

"I know," Ben groaned, and grabbed her arm for support.

"Jamie! Get the door!" Karen yelled.

Jamie moved toward the door, scanning the floor for a discarded weapon. The sound was intense, something he hadn't heard in a long time. He crouched as he went, and saw Billy shoot two of the Russians. *Good,* he thought. *Two less we have to worry about.*

He scooped up a pistol, checked to see if it was loaded, and continued to move.

⊶⊷

Karen took Ben's left hand and pressed it to his wound.

"Keep pressure on it. We're getting out of here," she said.

He looked at her and smiled. "I love you."

"I know," she replied, and smiled back as she turned away.

⊶⊷

Jamie saw Stephen shoot Dmitri out of the corner of his eye. He knew he had to move while others were occupied so he could get his friends out of here.

Billy was pushing more shells into the shotgun when he noticed Jamie. He looked frantically for the last Russian—he didn't want to be shot while trying to deal with Jamie. He brought the shotgun up to his shoulder and drew a bead on Jamie's back.

Karen was still close to Ben when she saw Billy taking aim.

"Jamie! Look out!" she shouted.

Billy fired. Two buckshot pellets from Billy's fire cut shallow grooves across Jamie's back. He fell to the floor, writhing in pain.

Billy grinned, cycled the pump shotgun, and took aim again to finish him off.

⊶⊷

The last Russian alive looked around the garage in disbelief. This was supposed to have been an easy job—take care of a few rednecks in Mississippi, nothing serious. Now two of his friends were dead and it looked like his boss was too.

He slammed another magazine into his rifle and peeked over the toolbox next to him. From this view, he could see Billy hiding behind the support that held up the lift where mechanics had once worked on cars. Billy looked like he was concentrating on shooting the young man moving across the floor at a low crouch.

He watched Billy fire once and the young man went down. The Russian took aim as Billy worked the action on his shotgun.

⚔️

Karen watched in horror as Jamie went down, and saw Billy behind the lift. She glanced at the toolbox next to the far wall and saw the Russian aiming at Billy.

"Jamie! Stay down!" she shouted. She ran to grab a pistol on the floor that one of Billy's men had dropped.

⚔️

Billy heard the woman shout and turned to face her. The boy looked like he was done. Plenty of time to finish him off after he took that bitch out.

His world exploded in pain as several bullets ripped through his cover and struck him in the chest. *Where the hell is that coming from?* he thought as he dropped.

As he fell, he saw the Russian firing at him and tried to point the shotgun in that direction. His shotgun's sights wavered around the Russian's face. Billy concentrated through the pain to hold the weapon steady and squeezed the trigger.

He was rewarded with a click.

Empty.

He groaned and allowed his head to hit the floor as he waited on the Russian to finish the job.

The Russian was confident now. He saw Billy take aim and try to shoot, but there was no action.

Ha! No more shells!

The Russian moved around the toolbox, keeping the rifle pointed at Billy.

I'll finish this one off, then the rest.

Karen slid in a pool of blood as she grabbed the pistol. Blood was everywhere, as well as a cloud of smoke from the excessive weapons fire.

She squinted to focus on the Russian, who was now walking toward Billy. She didn't give a shit about Billy, was in fact glad the man was out of the action.

What she didn't want was this Russian completing the job on the rest of them.

She kneeled and extended her arms, holding the pistol as steady as possible. The front sight was centered on the Russian's chest. She waited for him to stop moving before she fired.

The last Russian stood over Billy, watching Billy struggle to breathe through several holes in his chest. Billy's eyes were narrowed in pain as he looked up at his executioner.

"Just fuckin' do it already," Billy wheezed.

The Russian centered the rifle's sights on Billy's forehead and tightened his squeeze on the trigger.

He never completed this task. Two bullets hit him in the side of his head.

He fell across Billy, lifeless.

Billy couldn't make his arms work. He struggled to push himself out from beneath the Russian's body. Movement caught his eye, and he looked up to see Karen standing over him, pistol trained on his face.

CHAPTER THIRTY-ONE

*T*en feet.

It was only ten feet to the door. Stephen pushed himself along with his right arm, being careful not to move his left side. He was in agony, but knew he had to get out of here. He managed to get to his feet at the door and made his way outside, still clutching his pistol in his right hand.

＊＊＊

Ben saw Stephen go out the door.

Damn it, he thought. *There's no way you are getting away from me. Not after everything you've done.*

Ben stood, unsteadily at first. He saw Karen taking aim at the Russian and Jamie lying on the floor. He was torn between looking after his friends and going after Stephen. Jamie rolled over then and made eye contact with Ben. Jamie made a waving motion, implying *Go.*

Ben watched Karen shoot the Russian and move to cover Billy. He made his decision and moved out of the doorway to go after Stephen.

—⟨+ +⟩—

The blood was flowing now. Every step Ben took, he felt it running out of his side. He pressed his shirt against his ribs and continued to shuffle toward a nearby park.

He saw Stephen ahead of him going into the park. Stephen was also obviously in a bad way—he lurched from one side to another, his left arm dangling at his side. Ben could make out the outline of a pistol in his right hand.

Stephen entered the park, looked around, and hurried down the path.

"Stephen!" Ben shouted. "Stop!"

Ben saw Stephen's head cock, then his shoulders sagged. Stephen made his way toward a bench, turned, and collapsed into it. Ben walked toward him, his gun held in front of him.

"Just...stop, Stephen. Where are you going to go?"

Stephen looked up at Ben. He still held his own pistol in his right hand. He smiled.

"Well. Is this it? You got me, son. That's what you're expecting to hear, right?"

"Don't want to hear anything. Just sit there until somebody gets here to take you in."

Stephen shook his head. "Not going to jail, boy. Not an option."

"You see any other options right now?"

"Yes. You are going to shoot me and end all of this."

"I'm not going to shoot you, Stephen."

Stephen laughed. "Of *course* you're going to end this, son! I'm the bad guy, remember? You're the good guy! It's practically written in stone that you shoot me! I cannot be allowed to get away…that would completely destroy the narrative!"

Ben wavered. His head was screaming at him, his blood running out of the wound in his side, and he couldn't remember ever feeling this tired. *Narrative? What the fuck is* this *all about?*

"You've seen too many movies, Stephen. Reggie is on his way, or someone else, don't care at this point. You're going to be arrested. I ain't got time for any of this."

Stephen grinned. He glanced down at the pistol in his hand. The slide was locked to the rear, indicating an empty magazine. He returned his gaze to Ben.

"Allow an old man to talk. There is no way I can go to prison. There are enough people after me that I won't last a day if I'm detained. You've seen what money can do—that's what caused all of this. I'm telling you—I won't go to prison. *You* must kill me for this to end."

Ben sighed. "There's been enough killing. I don't want to kill you."

"Really? After all that's happened? After all I've done to you, you don't want to kill me? We aren't in the American South anymore, the whole eye for an eye thing? People are howling for my blood, you have a chance to actually carry out a justifiable killing, and you won't do it?"

"Seems to me that most folks who say they'd kill someone like you ain't never had blood on their hands. The ones who think they would be able to have never actually done it."

Ben winced as pain shot through his side. "Enough talking. Shut up and sit there."

Stephen laughed again. "Nice philosophy, Ben. Pity we never had the chance to sit down and talk. You have a lot of your father in you. Tell you what, I'll make it easy for you."

Still smiling, he pressed the magazine release on the side of his pistol. The empty magazine clattered to the pavement.

"What are you doing?" Ben asked.

"As I said, I'll make this easy for you."

Stephen felt underneath his jacket and retrieved another magazine for his pistol. It slipped from his grasp. He grunted, bent over, and picked it up.

Ben's vision swam. His side was on fire and freezing cold. A bolt of pain shot through his chest. His vision snapped back to full clarity as the pain continued all the way to his head.

He coughed. *Wonder if they got my lung too?*

"Let it go, Stephen."

"I can't, boy." He continued to smile as he finally grasped the magazine and maneuvered it to the butt of the pistol.

Shit. I don't want to kill him, he thought.

"Last chance, Ben. As soon as this pistol is loaded, you are going to die."

A long shadow appeared and disappeared on Stephen's face as blue and white strobes flashed through the park.

"Look at that. The law is here. No reason to do this. Just stop," Ben pleaded.

Ben heard the sirens and doors opening behind him. They sounded far away.

Stephen glanced over Ben's shoulder, then sagged against the bench, the pistol still in his grip.

"No. This is your decision, Ben. One way or another, this is it." He thumbed the slide release on the pistol and pointed it at Ben.

Ben shot him three times. He allowed the pistol to drop to his side as Stephen slumped against the metal bench, exhaling one last time.

Ben didn't think he had ever felt this tired in his life.

⭅₊ ₊⭆

Reggie and two deputies burst through the garage door. His eyes widened as he took the scene in before him.

Bodies lay in every corner. A thick pallor of smoke hung in the room, and the smell of blood and gunpowder was overwhelming. He saw Karen standing over someone, pointing a pistol, but couldn't see her intended target. He rushed to her side, looked down, and saw Billy.

Reggie reached out and grasped the pistol in her hand. "It's okay, Karen, it's okay," he whispered, and gently took it from her.

She looked at him for a moment, then nodded. "I'm fine, Reggie. I was just about to put this piece of shit out of his misery. Probably a good thing you just showed up." Her eyes widened, and she spun around. "Jamie! Get Jamie, he's hurt!"

"I'm all right," Jamie groaned as he sat up. Two deputies moved to his side to begin tending his wounds. One of the deputies grabbed his radio and called for paramedics.

Reggie looked around. "Good God," he murmured. "Who are all of these people? There were two that came after me and Linda. They all together?"

Karen nodded. She turned to go back to the corner where she left Ben, and saw he was gone.

"Oh shit," she breathed. "Ben's gone, I left him there. We have to go find him."

⊨═╬ ╬═⊨

Ben sat on the ground in front of the bench. He was exhausted and felt no need to move. He looked at Stephen's body, marveling that one man could have caused so much pain.

He heard running steps behind him and turned his head to see who it was.

Karen ran up and embraced him. Reggie came around to look at Stephen.

"You got him, huh?" Reggie said.

"Yeah," Ben replied. He thought for a second, then asked, "Is Linda okay?"

Reggie grunted. "She will be, eventually. I think we're all going to need some time to get over this."

Ben said nothing, and allowed Karen to hold him.

EPILOGUE

There are still thousands of small, non-chain motels and hotels in the country. Most people prefer to stay in the larger chains, as they provide more amenities, more security, and better service.

One of the benefits to the smaller, independent motels is not many ask for pesky things like identification or major credit cards. Most are grateful just to have the business, and cash is taken happily with few or no questions asked.

The man was staying in one of these in a very rural area of the South. The sign outside the motel still advertised color TV as one of the attractions. The TV worked, which is really all the man wanted.

He was stepping out of the shower when the local news channel began a breaking news segment. The man continued drying himself as he walked out of the bathroom and sat on the bed to watch.

"Violence in northern Mississippi tonight—Black Creek, Mississippi is a small town near the University of Mississippi, and earlier this evening was the scene of horrific violence as several unidentified people engaged in a gunfight. We go live to the scene now..."

The man watched as several witnesses were interviewed, describing the sounds of gunfire and how this sort of thing never happened in their town. The man grunted—that was an understatement. Nothing of interest *ever* happened there.

He bolted up and moved closer to the screen. The sheriff was being interviewed, but what had caught his eye was the person being put into an ambulance behind the sheriff, accompanied by a woman he didn't recognize.

He recognized the man in the ambulance. It's hard not to recognize your own son, even if you haven't seen him in years.

William Martin shook his head. *Good God, son, what have you gotten yourself into?*

ABOUT THE AUTHOR

W. L. Harvey spent six years serving in the US Navy and fifteen years with the US Army. He deployed five times with the Combined Joint Special Operations Task Force to Afghanistan and three times to conduct counterterrorism operations in South America.

Harvey retired in 2011. He now lives in Fayetteville, North Carolina, with his wife and dog. Harvey enjoys competitive shooting, exercising, gunsmithing, and writing. His thriller, *Back Home*, is set in an area similar to his hometown in rural Mississippi.